RED STATION

KENZIE JENNINGS

DEATH'S HEAD PRESS

an imprint of Dead Sky Publishing, LLC
Miami Beach, Florida
www.deadskypublishing.com

ISBN: 9781639510368

First Edition

Cover Art: Justin T. Coons

The "Splatter Western" logo designed
by K. Trap Jones

Book Layout: Lori Michelle
www.TheAuthorsAlley.com

For Amanda, who'd make the greatest final girl in a Splatter Western.

SUNDOWN

IT WAS THE hour of fresh blood, and the land was ravenous.

The man staggered out onto the muddy field, shaking his head at the persistent, low drone in his ears, a weak attempt to shake it loose. To a casual observer, he may have looked a sight akin to a town drunkard weaving and shuffling his woozy way back home on the edge of the badlands after another raucous night in the saloon. Had the outsider taken one step closer, perhaps the man could have possibly been saved from the wild, from the elements.

From himself.

Alas, the man was alone there. His movements grew heavy with each step, his legs lifting and trembling as if weighed down by stones in his shoes, the mud squelching beneath them. He stepped forward again and swayed. His blurry gaze locked on the scene ahead of the weak, sinking sun, a murky golden orb settling down on the line of the vast horizon.

The shadows stretched their arms as the last sliver of light said goodbye to the man whose mouth had dropped open. A thin thread of bloody spittle hung from his open lips, threatening to fall. He came to a

1

wobbly halt, his breath caught in his throat. A new stream of blood trickled down his forehead from the top of his skull, a sticky rivulet that just made it down to his right eyelid before it caught in his lashes. He rapidly blinked, trying to rid his eyes of the stickiness, the one action he could muster without too much difficulty in the moment. He then weakly raised a hand to his forehead, trailing his fingers over the stickiness. The blood, it kept coming, rolling down his forehead, forming branches of rivers.

For a minute, he felt along his head, his fingers probing, seeking the injury. It didn't hurt anywhere at all. If anything, his whole head felt numb and springy, nothing more. His fingers, however, found the source of the blood, a deep indented wound in the center of the top of his skull, hot and oozing with pulp. He drew his hand away, examining it closely. His fingertips were coated in dark clots and wiry strands of hair clung to the gore on his middle finger.

The man had no idea what had happened to him, how he'd obtained the injury. He couldn't recall anything whatsoever, nothing of significance in the mush of his brain. His memory had grown fuzzy, its imagery dipped in a red haze.

Just then, the night howled, a baying, mournful sound that startled the man out of his thoughts. The sound was joined by another, then another, and yet another, until the coyote chorus had taken over the night with its concerto grosso. Perhaps whatever existed there on the way back would grant him answers as to the how's, the where's, and the why's.

Perhaps whatever existed there on the way back

would be safer than out in the middle of the wide open where he was potential prey.

The man wavered, turned back around, and was struck hard by something with immense force. He staggered backwards, tottering, blinking at the sudden deluge of blood, like sticky tar, pouring, curtaining down from the gaping wound in his forehead. He tried to form words, attempting to speak out, his voice coming in a stream of incoherent muttering.

When he was struck again, everything went silent, and the pitch chewed him whole.

ONE

SHE WORE RED well, a deep, rich red much like garnet.

It was what the good doctor first noticed of her when she primly sat across from him in the stagecoach carriage, smoothing her skirts down as she did. It was a bold color, not normally chosen for rough rides across the pitted plains. She was out of her element there, it seemed. A lady of refined society, one more inclined to find herself at ease at evening soirees. Everything, from the color and tucked and nipped style of her wear to the odd accessory touches she had on her person, like the parasol with the silver engraved handle and the tinted spectacles, spoke of an eccentric elegance, one that would undoubtedly cease to find suitable home amongst the settlers there. She had spent much of the journey engrossed in her book, her gaze occasionally drifting from the yellowing pages (a book that had been read again and again, he'd surmised) to the scene of the rolling landscape beside her moving along at a bumpy, swaying clip.

When the doctor finally held her stare, locking it in with his own, she closed the book, and offered him a tight smile, one that held no promises or potentials.

The young, rosy woman seated beside her was still sleeping, softly snoring, her head tucked at a painfully unnatural angle against the side panel, the curtain bunched at her side. They'd all agreed during the journey to have two of the curtains rolled down for the day as the sun's rays that had been coming in on one side were powerful enough to form beads of sweat. The doctor had offered his seatmate, the girl's husky bear of a husband, an extra handkerchief he'd kept on his person, and the bear gratefully took it and blotted at his damp brow. He'd tried to give it back to the doctor, but the doctor insisted the bear keep it. It wasn't as if he'd not prepared enough for the journey ahead. The doctor had known the land, its climate, and its people well enough to come along with essentials.

After all, the doctor could possibly be returning from this route with another, dead or alive. Better alive, of course, but if so, it was prudent of him to carry several of the bare necessities, including handkerchiefs.

The lady in red set her book aside and rummaged in her beaded handbag, a colorful item at odds with her dress' monochromatic style. She pulled out a tortoiseshell hand fan, flicked it open, and cooled herself with it, carefully avoiding the pull of the doctor's stare. He was handsome, she supposed, if that sort of meticulous gentleman's cut and trim he presented was to one's fancy. She often paid little attention to such details in a possible suitor, preferring the quiet company of solitude. Even still, long travel times in such close quarters would inevitably lead to exchange with fellow travelers, anything to idle away the time.

They had stopped to stretch their legs and relieve themselves once that day, their destination for the evening a mere few hours' journey. It was a home station their driver, a jaunty young fellow by the strangely antipodal name of Moody Evers, had prattled on about, something about the hostess' crumb cake and the downy bedding there. It would be a welcome respite where they could get their bearings for the remainder of the journey. The closer they came to their destination, the cheerier they grew. Even Leartus, the surly, iron-jowled shotgun, had halted the acidic comebacks towards his young cohort who'd tried (and apparently hadn't learned) throughout the journey to engage him in small talk.

The carriage suddenly jolted, causing the girl who had been sleeping to wake with a start. Her leg kicked against the rumpled skirts of the lady in red, the side of her hard shoe making brief contact with something solid. Underneath all of that material, it was difficult to tell unless one were inclined to make eye contact with the owner of the skirts as the girl eventually did, her cheeks going pink with embarrassment.

"Beg pardon, ma'am," she said with a nervous chuckle, her hand out and patting down the lady's dress. "Sometimes, the pull of the sheep sends me off, right to black, and the devil shakes me wide awake with a start so's I've no idea where I am."

The lady in red returned the girl's chortle, instantly softening the moment.

"That you can fall soundly asleep here is remarkable. Truthfully," she said, putting her book down. She then leaned to the side, her splayed fan at the side of her mouth as if she was about to share a secret between them. " . . . I can't abide these sorts of journeys in such tight quarters. Like we're all trapped in a hot box that rattles and sways at the slightest hitch in the trail."

"Yet you're able to ease your jangled nerves by reading on a stage," said the doctor. "How's *that* not remarkable?"

"I find reading soothing, almost meditative."

"May I ask what it is you're reading that has you soothed?"

There was a mocking lilt in his tone the lady in red didn't much care for, as if he'd found it silly, frivolous even, that she'd find some solace in words on a page. Still, she thought, it would be awfully fun to engage his interest with a bit of a shock. She had placed the book on the seat in her lap face down, so she then picked it up and held it up for him to see for himself.

"*A Vindication of the Rights of Woman,*" he read from its cover. "Is it a persuasive treatise? A call to action?"

"A response," she said flatly.

"A response to . . . ?"

"To those who believe women should not be expected to be rational thinkers."

He was silent for a moment, seeming to absorb what she'd said, before responding with "Why on earth would one believe that? I've never once found women irrational or illogical. Individuals, yes, of course. But to establish this as a thesis for an entire sex, it's absurd."

"Well, I dunno about that," mused the big man, a twinkle dancing his eye. "Been around plenty a'gals who'd take a good look at the sun during the day t'see if it was still there, blindin' themselves right quick when they did."

The girl across from him gasped in mock dismay and then playfully smacked his knee. "Finch Henry, you lie like a dirty rug!"

"I ain't lyin', girl. You try lookin' direct at the sun n'see what happens."

"Fool. You're lyin' when you said you been around plenty girls," she quipped. "Ain't a girl from Topeka to Cowtown that woulda given you the time of day."

"So you're Mr. Finch Henry," said the doctor, turning to look at his seatmate. "We'd all been so immersed in our own thoughts and affairs, we'd neglected pleasantries altogether. Montgomery Pickering." He held out a hand for the big man who shook it, enveloping the doctor's hand in his bear paw.

"It's Finch Henry Wilkson, sir," he said gruffly, shaking the proffered hand. "Henry's my papa's name he give me to use only when formality was necessary. And for my mama to use when I done somethin' she didn't much care for."

"He done a *lot* a things she didn't much care for," the girl said with a smirk in her husband's direction. "Marryin' me was one."

That elicited a laugh from everyone in the little group. Even the quiet lady in red chuckled politely.

"And what is your name, young lady, or will Mrs. Wilkson suit? I ask in courtesy to your preference," said the doctor.

The girl wasn't sure if it was the question or the doctor's honeyed tenor that caused her to cheeks and neck to flush. She wasn't used to such silken speech, from a gentleman nonetheless. "I . . . You . . . You can call me Patience, Mr. Pickering sir."

"That would be *Doctor* Pickering, if one were to adhere to social conventions and proper titles, but since I'm on personal business, and we're to the acquaintance stage of our journey, please call me Monty." He flashed a look in the lady in red's direction. "Montgomery, if you'd prefer, of course."

But the lady in red chose to ignore Monty, her eyes drawn to Patience's hands fidgeting in her lap like nervous, fluttering, little birds. She patted the girl's knee and then placed a warm hand over the girl's own, stilling the movement.

"Not a traveler, are you?" she asked the girl.

Patience stared hard at the lady's hand over hers, both uncertain as to how to explain herself and surprised at the audacity of her forward seatmate. "No, ma'am. Not really," she managed with a half-chuckle. "Not used to fancy neither."

"What's 'fancy' about any of this?" the lady in red said, a playful scoff in her tone.

Patience eyed her seatmate's hand and finery, signaling her meaning. "Ain't 'what's' fancy," she remarked. "It's *'who's'* fancy."

The lady in red removed her hand, releasing its light trap over Patience's. She brushed down her skirts, her own nervous habit, the doctor surmised. Their eyes met once again, his own teasing her to answer, hers daring him to break away.

She simply hadn't the inclination for pleasantries. Her focus was elsewhere than on the journey itself. She then realized the silence among the group, everyone else's focus curiously on her.

"I'm not here to break bread," she said. "However, as we will be corralled for the night, I suppose it will be to our benefit to learn names, especially when calling for assistance in the late hours." She sighed before continuing, holding out her hand in the doctor's direction. They shook hands. "Clyde Northway, soon to be Darrow."

Monty seemed to flinch, drawing his hand away. "As in Commodore Darrow?"

"The very same."

"See?" piped in Patience, who nodded knowingly at her husband. "Fancy."

"Pardon my ignoramus," said Finch, "but who's that?"

But both Monty and Clyde had grown quiet, the doctor still evidently stunned at the revelation.

He finally managed to swallow down the stone that had caught in his throat before he answered. "That would be Commodore John T. Darrow of the James River Squadron. Old money in his lineage. People have said he'd enjoyed the fight, took pleasure in it. Though it's been also said by many he'd gone blood mad when Admiral Semmes ordered his ship destroyed. It was only to evade capture, you understand."

"So, he's out *here*?" said Patience. She looked from Monty to Clyde, then back again, attempting to gauge where the answer lay.

Monty nodded, continuing, "After the war, the Commodore had reportedly traveled west. There's word of him having purchased the entirety of a town, its land wholly his, not far from our stay. Perhaps another day's travel from there."

11

"Idlecreek. He oversees Idlecreek," Clyde said, cutting Monty's exposition. She'd simply wished for him to cease talking altogether.

But he didn't. She should have known better than to ride with a man in a suit. They talked more than she'd cared for.

"I don't mean to be forward," he said, "but I'd heard he'd had . . . *troubles* . . . with . . . well, with women and gunfights, that sort of carousing quite akin to what has ailed Dodge City. A lady with your stature and grace may sway him a different course. Although, there's the rub in his habits alone."

"Ah, but you see you *did* mean to be forward," she replied. "And I needn't remind you that it *isn't* gentlemanly to engage in empty gossip. You're not part of a sewing circle, after all. Or are you, Dr. Pickering? Chew the rag to wile away the hours with the ladies?"

That elicited a titter from the other two passengers who exchanged a look between them. It was the doctor's turn to flush red from the top of his head to his neckline.

"If I've offended," he said, "good lady, I am sorry. I simply wished to convey my concern—"

Clyde waved his words off, a simple gesture to indicate it wasn't necessary for him to finish. "And I apologize, too, for my terseness. Your concern is appreciated, truly. I'm more than aware of Commodore Darrow's previously held appetites, as others have warned as well."

"How did you meet him?" asked Patience. She had a dreamy look on her face, as if she was in another world, one where ladies were swept off their feet by rough riders, men who'd simply lost their way.

"A correspondence in the *Matrimonial Times*. We've exchanged letters over the months. His prose is careful and concise, prosaic, and yet there's a certain loveliness about it, revealing an absolute gentleman. He proposed, and by then, I knew it was right. So I accepted, and here I am."

"You never met each other? This'll be your first time?"

"Patience, that ain't none o'your business," chided Finch.

"I don't mind," said Clyde. "No, we've not set eyes on each other, but that's about to change now, isn't it?"

Finch beamed at her, his grin taking over his face. "Well, many congratulations to you and yours, ma'am. Patience and me been wedded . . . what . . . two months now?"

"It's round about," added Patience, returning her husband's smile. "We're joinin' my folks in Fredonia. They got them a nice piece a'land. Big barn. Cows. Plenty chickens."

"Good place to raise babies," said Finch.

Patience patted her belly. "A good . . . *good* place."

Clyde and Monty exchanged a glance before turning back to their seatmates.

"You're having a baby? That's wonderful," said Monty at the same time as Clyde said, "Many congratulations to you as well."

Patience flushed a lovely shade of pink, smiling, and Finch laughed at the sight of her blushing. "Lookit her. She gone all soft n'sweet-like."

"That sort of happiness, it suits," murmured Clyde. "Changes the way about you, like you're alight."

Finch leaned across, took his wife's hands in his own, and kissed them one at a time. A sweet, simple gesture.

The little group had been quiet for a good while, the muggy air having lulled the married couple to a semi-lethargic state. However, Clyde and Monty had not taken to the pull of the afternoon. Both were still awake, alert and focused.

"Any idea how much longer gonna take t'get there?" Patience murmured.

Finch let out a lion's yawn, taking care not to unfold his legs in a stretch. "We'll be there shortly, my lovely. Cain't be much longer." A grin played across his broad face and he winked slyly at Clyde, who smiled in turn before honing her sights again on the doctor.

"You mentioned you were on personal business. Is it the sort that involves land, family, marriage, or . . . " She let her pause hang there in implication.

The doctor's eyes gleamed. "Or?"

"Choose your vice, doctor. A secret lover? A debt? Old wounds? Betrayal, revenge . . . *murder*?"

The sudden silence emanating from the doctor was jagged in its cut. Patience glanced, wide-eyed, at her husband, who shifted uncomfortably in his seat, taking great pains not to accidentally move his leg in the wrong direction, right up against the doctor's. Since the poor man's bulk practically consumed half of the carriage's interior, this was a difficult feat for him, and inevitably, as he moved, he pivoted his knee against the doctor's own, the awkward movement causing the doctor to be shaken from his silence.

Monty reached deep into his waistcoat pocket and pulled out a ferrotype photograph. He held it out for Clyde, who took it and examined it with a concentrated scowl that lined her normally smooth face. Patience leaned in to get a good look at it as well.

The image on it was of a lanky man sitting on a high-backed chair. A toothy girl no more than a sprite with a pinafore over gingham dress, pigtail plaits, and a playful smirk stood beside the man. A somber dark-haired beauty of a woman stood behind the girl, her hand on her husband's shoulder. Her clear gaze was strong and assured in the photographer's direction.

"That . . . is Mr. George Fancher, his wife Elise who passed on mere weeks after that was taken, and their only child, Catherine. Mrs. Fancher was a patient of mine, one I was unable to cure due to the severity of her condition, but I was, at least, able to bestow some comfort for her during her final days. It's the blessing and curse of the profession."

"I can only imagine," Clyde said softly. Her eyes met the doctor's. He seemed to be seeking something in the two women, his gaze intently flickering between Clyde and Patience, who gently pried the ferrotype from Clyde's grip to examine it more closely.

"I've held a brotherly acquaintance with Mr. Fancher since, and while our meetings were limited due the distance between our residences—he being a man of the land while I'd settled comfortably in town with my practice—we discovered a mutual interest in bridge, something I'd picked up years ago from a lady I'd been quite fond of. Very nearly engaged to.

Anyway, Mr. Fancher and his daughter would join me and another friend in my parlor to partake in a game or two. He'd taught Cat when she was no more than four or five, and she turned out to be quite the card player."

"Why do you carry this with you?" Patience asked as she handed the ferrotype to the doctor, who promptly tucked it back inside his waistcoat.

"Patience, there comes a point where a man don't need to explain the nature of his habits and idiosyncratics," chided Finch. "Sorry, doc. She gets all spun-crazy in curiosity. Just how she is."

"Well, I *am* the one who showed it to her," reminded the doctor. "It would be impolite *not* to explain or offer context of some sort." He then turned his attention to Patience. "I carry it with me for the very reason I revealed it to you. To see if there was some sort of recognition in your eyes, your body language."

"You're looking for them, your friend and his daughter?" said Clyde.

That instantly woke Patience alert, her interest suddenly peaked. "What? What happened to them?"

"That, I have yet to ascertain, Mrs. Wilkson. Mr. Fancher's plan was to settle north, taking this route, but that was some time ago. None of their neighbors or local family members have heard from them. Mr. Fancher's sister requested someone search for their whereabouts, and I gladly obliged. I fear they encountered trouble on their journey."

"You oughtta ask if the driver or shotgun seen 'em," said Finch.

"No need. Neither of them has any idea."

Patience had gone ashen at his words. "Could be Injuns. You think they got 'em? I heard some of them collect scalps, an' others even eat their own babies." The very thought of it had Patience cupping her hands protectively over her belly. "Or maybe some of them bandits that been hidin' out here," she added.

"Girl, you know not to pay no mind to my papa's taradiddles an' prejudicials," said Finch. "He only tells 'em when he wants to set the young 'uns right, scarin' 'em off the trail. Keeps 'em all from strayin' too far from home."

"Well, it worked, didn't it? Now they're all scared stupid to leave the house!"

"Exactly. An' if they don't leave home, Papa don't have to worry none about the rest'a them movin' away like the two of us, leavin' him an' mama alone to keep the farm goin'.'"

"You ain't gonna guilt me none about it, Finch *Henry*. We got to do things on our own now that we're married and gonna have ourselves a baby."

"An' that's why we're movin' straight from my family to yours, doin' things on 'our own'," muttered Finch.

"You sassin' me, husband?"

"No, ma'am. I was just sayin'—"

"Cause it sure sounds like some prickly sass comin' from that seat."

Finch turned towards his seat partner, his eyes pleading for support from a potential brother-in-arms.

"Don't look to me for empathy, my good man," chortled Monty. "I've been so graciously deemed a 'bachelor-for-life' by generally well-intentioned

17

cohorts and siblings, a title that carries little respect in this area of the country."

"I'm curious, doctor," Clyde interjected. "What do *you* think may have happened to them?"

He cleared his throat loudly and straightened further in his seat. He'd grown flustered by both the intensity of her stare boring into his cache of secrets as well as the thought that he'd revealed far too much to strangers in such a short amount of time. When Monty met her eyes again, the lady in red visibly softened, relaxing her shoulders, easing her smile. *She* understood him, even empathized with him despite norms and conventions of the day, so at the very least, she could broach this issue that had been weighing heavily on his conscience for some time with gentility and grace, and since the man read body language, she'd use it to her advantage.

Still, Clyde was certain there was, perhaps, much more to the good doctor than he projected, and since there was enough time to wile away, she thought it engaging conversation that would keep the young couple's marital banter at bay. As amusing as it was, there was only so much of it one could take before it grew tedious.

Monty took in a breath and exhaled slowly, deeply, before continuing. "I have my suspicions, Miss Northway, none of which involve scalping anyone or eating babies." He lobbed that one specifically at Patience, whose complexion turned a pale pink, hot-cheeked in embarrassment. "If such news holds any sort of value, aside from bee patter, there have been several travelers on this *particular* route who have gone missing, and there is no sole commonality of note among them."

"What are your suspicions then, doctor?" pressed Clyde.

"I was just going to add they've no single common trait aside from items of value they carried on their journeys. Trinkets, deeds, bonds, family troves. Those travelers were all intent upon new lives, new beginnings." He looked at Patience, nodding grimly at her. "Therefore, I'm inclined to agree with you, Mrs. Wilkson. These scoundrels . . . they're thieves. However, they are not bandits or any sort of . . . *highwaymen* I'm remotely familiar with. Look out there. There is no certain area in which to hide."

"No matter, you don't worry yourself 'bout nothin', lovely," Finch said to his wife. "Them thieves an' bushwackers gonna be a mite disappointed. We ain't got much to pilfer aside from some Sunday clothes an' baby toys."

"Your mama's baby rattle," murmured Patience.

"Girl, that thing ain't real silver. My mama got it in her head she owns a worldly treasure in that there baby toy, claimin' it's been passed down 'til it tarnished."

"If it's *tarnished*, it's more likely *real* silver, now, ain't it?"

"If they want the damned thing, they can have it, all I care."

Patience gasped, mortified. "Finch *Henry*. Mind your manners n' hold your tongue."

At that, Finch made a show of sticking out his tongue and grasping it with his hand, crossing his eyes at Patience as he did.

Before everyone could share a laugh and relax a bit, there was a sharp whistle and shout from the whip, and they suddenly froze, exchanging startled looks, realizing something at the same time as the other.

"Why, ladies and gentlemen," said Monty, his grin breaking loose. "I believe we've reached our destination."

TWO

"**BEAUTIFUL DAY IN** God's country," chirped Moody, the driver, as he helped his passengers step down from the carriage one at a time. "Leartus gonna stay in the Adlers' stable tonight, keep watch over the horses, help out their hostler. I'll be your introductions n'all. Oh, careful now. Watch yer feet, ma'am. Must've rained mud all week."

Clyde stepped carefully over the puddle Moody pointed out for her. While the sun was merely a murky sliver on the horizon, its fading fingers continued to caress the damp, heady plains, teasing the possibility of nightfall. Dark storm clouds were rolling in, readying themselves to take control of the evening.

There was a trickle of rain. Clyde held out her hand to it, palm up, and a fat raindrop splashed in the center. She then swiftly opened her parasol and held it over her head, squinting at the house at the end of the muddy path.

It was a strange, two-story monstrosity of a building, as if its owners felt announcing to the empty landscape that they were settling, by gum, and they would build what amounted to the rugged equivalent of a manor house but without all the frivolous trimmings. After all, one couldn't seem too ostentatious out in "God's country." That aside, the odd estate—with its main house, stables, carriage house, sod-walled corral, outbuilding, and storage cistern—was a stark beacon against the vast emptiness of the plains. There seemed to be no neighbors in the vicinity, just ever-rolling pastures.

The wind skirled, and thunder rumbled in the distance. It was the only sound of the plains, but it sent a shiver creeping down Clyde's back. Someone said something behind her, and she whirled around, trying to catch the words hanging there for her to comprehend and then answer.

"What was that?" she said, suddenly turning right into Monty.

The doctor laughed, catching her by the arm as she swayed on her feet. "Careful now. Gives one a dizzy spell, that never-ending, circular pull of the land with the wind in one's ears."

"Forgive me, I don't—" She patted his hand, signaling for him to let go, and he did, but not without reservation, for he remained right at her side. She shooed him away. "I'm quite all right. I've been so attuned to the sights and sounds of the city, I'd forgotten what it was like out here in the wide open."

The wind whipped and snatched with its greedy hands, shrieking its rage at the little group, and promptly turned Clyde's parasol inside out.

"Oh, for God's sake," she snapped as she attempted to right it back.

However, the wind had other ideas and smacked roughly at her skirts, flattening their bulk against her back. Her hat, having been pinned meticulously down, loosened from her hair and flapped, threatening to leave its spot. She dropped her carpetbag on the ground and grasped her hat with the hand not bearing the inside-out parasol.

"Mr. Evers! Would you mind assisting? I've another bag aboard!" she shouted against the gale.

Moody had heard absolutely nothing though, having turned his focus on unloading the baggage from the roof of the carriage for his passengers to carry as Leartus barked something at him from the other side of the stage beside the horses.

The others fared no better against the wind. The doctor lost his own hat to the force of the wind, and he'd gone after it, chasing it as it bobbed and swirled in the air. Clyde could hear him laughing at the absurdity of it, lightening the mood for her as she juggled with her own belongings. She squinted against the wind, her eyes watering as she did, catching the blurry sight of several figures gathered in front of the house's entrance. One of them raised a hand high in the air. It looked as if the figure was signaling something to them, but she couldn't be sure.

One of the figures made a sound that was captured and swallowed by the wailing wind. The sun had sunk into the line of the horizon, having waved a bleak goodbye, and Clyde watched as the thunderheads rolled in, their grousing foreshadowing a night's worth of clamor.

"Best be gettin' up to the big house!" Moody shouted in her ear, causing Clyde to jump. He picked up her bag, performing a balancing act as he juggled carrying several other bags as well. "Storm's gonna break the ground, make all kinda trouble, but Leartus don't wanna come in! I keep tellin' him he can't stay in the stable on a night like this!"

"He should be fine!" Clyde shouted back, beckoning him onward beside her as they made their way to the house. "He's hale and hearty. As long as he has shelter, a roof over him. To further note, we're not on high ground!"

"Blessings to the good Lord above we're not!"

"The Lord has nothing to do with it. Thank our station hosts for the shelter for everyone!"

"Beg pardon, ma'am, if it weren't for His almighty power, our hosts wouldn't exist, would they?" quipped Moody as he kept along with her steady stride.

"I don't have the time or inclination to argue beliefs of which came first, the chicken or the egg, Mr. Evers! Not when your good Lord above seems quite incensed about something!"

"Whaddaya mean? What's He angry about this time?"

"I don't know, Mr. Evers! Our very existence perhaps? We've treated this land so well thus far, haven't we? Even those of us with no family, alone in this world. We've no excuse for this all. We are *all* responsible!"

"You an orphan, Miss Northway?"

Clyde side-eyed him, giving him a smirk. "Born and bred!"

It took Moody a moment to catch on, but when he did, he laughed, a short yap, and led her up the stairs of the main house's entrance just when a snap-crack of thunder lashed out from behind them. He then dropped the luggage upon the stairs that let out a creaking groan underneath the bulky weight.

But Clyde was already back in formal guise, standing there stiffly, waiting for proper introductions. She wasn't about to set foot inside without officially meeting the owners of the home where they were staying for the night.

There were two of them there, talking with the Wilksons who'd somehow managed to get up to the house quickly against the wind. They were an earthy stock of a man and woman, both of that sort of indeterminate age between 45 and 65, the climate having weathered and toughened their skin like rawhide. The man's height was imposing, much like Finch's stature, but unlike Finch, the man was a stone fortress looming over his guests. His face, however, belied his body's stature, for while his frame was stiff and solid, his face was doughy, his cheeks chubby, and his chin and jaws overgrown with beard. His wide-set grey eyes flinted from one guest to the next, as if taking in the details of them, and his smile was warm and welcoming.

The woman was also quite tall, a full foot taller than Clyde and Moody. She was almost as stocky as the man standing beside her. She made eye contact with Clyde and self-consciously patted back and preened at the stray strands of hair escaping from her loose, greying bun wrapped at the back of her head. It was often the case with women around Clyde, instantly seeming to gauge their adequacy when faced with a woman who appeared to have means, so Clyde decided to soften the woman a bit by mirroring her actions, patting down her own hairstyle and pinning back her own loose strands that had escaped in the wind. It helped. Both women tittered at the sheer absurdity of the matter, the very idea of attempting to pit fashion against the gale.

"Mr. Schurchell is tending to the team in this, ever the dutiful madman. How on earth . . . ?" panted the doctor from behind them, who then took the stairs two at a time, breathless as he did. "I doubt very much he'll be joining us this evening, despite the weather. Is it always like this out here?" he said in Moody's direction. "I don't remember this area being quite so prone to such dastardly winds."

"Oh, this is the prairie, sir," said the fortress, his voice a low, melodic grumble of a sound that entranced the ears. "There be no consistence here. One day, blasted storms; the next, calm and quiet as a baby's sighs." He offered a hand for the doctor. "Pleasure is ours to have you here. Welcome."

Monty shook the fortress' hand, one with a solid grip, firm and assured. He drew his hand away with a wince and a chortle. "That's quite a handshake you have, sir. Man of the soil. I confess I'm merely one of human study. Doctor Montgomery Pickering."

The fortress narrowed his eyes at the doctor, as if examining him further upon learning of Monty's profession, nodding in greeting as he did. The rest of the party awkwardly waited for further introductions, the whips of the wind the only sound there.

Finally, Moody cleared his throat and said, "Suppose it's on me then to make the formalities. Folks, this is Mr. an' Mrs. Adler, our hosts for the evenin.' Been told times over they've a mighty fine sup' an' bed for travelers along this way." He then went around the group, pointing each out to the host couple as he did. "Mr. and Mrs. Wilkson here are newlyweds on their way to their homestead. You've been introduced to Dr. Pickering there. And this here is Miss Northway, 'bout to exchange nuptials over in Idlecreek with the great Commodore Darrow himself."

That last introduction was enough to cause some curiosity to flash in their hosts' eyes. Mrs. Adler seemed particularly interested. It wasn't as if Clyde hadn't felt the heat of the big woman's stare. They'd exchanged a nervous laugh before, seeming to relax a bit in the other's presence, but afterwards, Mrs. Adler had chosen to ignore the other men, keeping her gaze locked on Clyde during Moody's introductions.

"The name's Moody Evers," the young man said, his freckled face beaming sunshine. He held out a hand for Mr. Adler. "I tell you, I been waitin' for a route out here just for this stop on the way. I dunno if you remember, but Finn Dugey's a friend o'mine. He was out here 'bout two months back on a mail run, an' he said you were the most hospitable folks with your home out here in the plains. 'Can't miss 'em,' he told me. 'They're in the big house that looks as if it's guardin' the land an' horizon. Got the best cake an' kirsch' . . . Issat how you say it? Kirsch? Don't rightly know 'bout *kirsch*, but Dugey brought me somma that cake, an' I tell you what, a little piece of pure heaven." He then directed his attention on Mrs. Adler who had gone tight-lipped with her smile. "Ma'am, might I say, your cookin' . . . You have a godly gift there."

Mrs. Adler shot him a quizzical frown. Her husband turned to her and said something to her in a language that was guttural and edged. When Mr. Adler caught the uncertainty in their body language,

27

their awkward smiles, their looks exchanged among each other, he laughed, a jolly, rumbling sound from deep within his belly.

"My wife," he said, playfully thumping Moody on the shoulder. "She speaks English, but it takes some time for her to understand everything you say. She will be slow to . . . how do you say it properly . . . She will be slow to 'catch up'? And she will be careful when she speaks to you." He turned back to her and said something else, and whatever it was, it made her light up, instantly brightening her tightly wound, stoic façade, creating pink blooms in her cheeks.

"Oh, yes, there is a *gut* meal for everyone," she said, carefully enunciating each word for them. "Please, come, come." She held the door open and beckoned them in. "The meal cooks, stays hot in . . . *Kanonenofen.* There is also soft beds, *und* my girls are happy to . . . ehm . . . make baths for you."

"Oh, Lord, how I would *love* a soak," murmured Patience as she followed everyone in.

"Girls? Finn never said nothin' about 'em. I've a mind t'have words with him whenever I see him again," Moody said with a nervous chuckle.

Patience gripped her husband's coat sleeve, in awe of the place. "I ain't never seen a house like this 'cept in picture books. Mayor back home had the biggest place, but it weren't nothin' like this one."

"Oh, I dunno, lovely," her husband said, his eyes half on her and half on the paintings decorating the walls. "We could build somethin' bigger now. Maybe big enough to hold all the babies we gonna have, givin' 'em some room to play." He faced Mr. Adler who towered there, blocking off the doorway to what looked to be a parlor of some sort but was so shrouded in darkness; it was difficult to tell.

The little group stood in the center of the narrow entryway that poured into a curved foyer that held a winding flight of stairs with heavy wooden railings leading up to the second floor. The foundation of the house, as solidly built as it seemed, creaked and whistled, the wind rattling its windows. Dark clouds had since rolled in across the wide expanse of sky, throwing its shadow over the house. The only light inside came from the soft glow of the oil lamps from their cast iron wall mounts.

Mrs. Adler snapped what sounded like a brittle command over her shoulder, and two young women emerged from what looked to be a cave of a kitchen at the rear of the first-floor landing. One of them, fair-haired and pretty, had a light in her eye, a twinkle of perpetual amusement. She looked to be around twenty or so, her willowy figure a stark contrast to Mrs. Adler's stout frame. She held herself assuredly, her poise proud, her head high. She was even dressed as if she'd been waiting for guests to appear, all in blue bows and silk draping, her bustle jostling from behind.

The other couldn't have been more than fifteen or so, a shy mouse in comparison to her counterpart. While the older of the two had her golden curls in a fashionable updo, the quiet one had her hair in a loose braid over her shoulder, straggles of dishwater hair barely curtaining one side of her face. Her gingham dress was pressed and plain with a stained apron covering its front.

What was the most startling about the younger

woman's appearance was the way her mouth seemed to be permanently twisted to one side, as if invisible hooks were tugging at it, pulling it aside. Her grey eyes fleetingly snuck a glimpse in Mrs. Adler's direction, as if willing her for permission to even consider looking at their guests. Clyde caught it, only just, and was momentarily startled at the girl's eyes. The irises were so pale, they seemed as ghostly as the girl herself, blending, merging with her snowy skin. Mrs. Adler shook her head, her lips tightly shut, at the girl, a signal they'd evidently practiced with time, for the girl bowed her head and scurried up the staircase.

While that particularly odd moment had been happening, the men in among the travelers had fallen under the spell of the other young woman and her easy charm. She held out a graceful hand to the doctor, her smile coy and practiced.

"Lovely to meet you. Welcome to our humble palace among the savages," she said with a merry twinkle in her eye. "Although the only savages we've encountered on our travels have been of the brawling, whiskey-imbibing sort, and thankfully, they've been but few."

Monty took her hand in his own, his smile meeting his eyes. "Thank the heavens for it, or you wouldn't have graced us with your presence as you are. Dr. Montgomery Pickering. An absolute pleasure."

He then bent to kiss her hand, an act that elicited a slight sneer from Clyde, who then smoothly held out her own in the young woman's direction.

"Since we're in the midst of such formalities," she said, aiming that in Monty's general direction, "Thank you kindly for your hospitality. It's most appreciated. Been quite an arduous day."

The young woman managed to break her gaze away from the doctor's own to meet Clyde's, and Clyde caught a flash of something so fleeting there, something deep and dark but too far-reaching for Clyde to be certain of what she saw. Instead, Clyde was greeted with the same warmth and elegant ease as the young woman beamed at her and shook her hand. Even the young woman's handshake felt off, lacking in something Clyde couldn't pinpoint. Her chilly, dry fingers coiled around Clyde's hand, trapping it briefly, even a bit painfully, just before she released her grip.

"Of course. Of course," said the young woman. "It's the primary reason why we've settled out here to begin with, in God's land, our own household a haven for those far from home." She nodded in the group's general direction. "Or, perhaps, for those seeking a home, if you are in fact. Though heaven only knows why here of all places when there is plenty to be mined elsewhere."

"God's land is rich in stock," quipped Moody, his boyish grin attempting to dazzle. It was his turn to hold out a hand in her direction. "I'm not as cultivated-like as the good doctor. If anything, am a mite bashful whenever pretty girls make my acquaintance. Moody Evers, miss, and might I say, you are a plumb sight for the weary. An angel in such finery if I ever seen."

"Charmed, Mr. Evers. Thank you for the compliment. I'm blushing. Truly." The young woman shook his hand, returning his grin.

In that moment, Clyde could've sworn she saw something pass between the two of them, some flicker of acknowledgment, perhaps. She wasn't entirely sure, but she wasn't ever inclined to doubt her instincts. After all, they had allowed her to survive for as long as she had.

The young lady then turned back to Clyde, eyes dancing in amusement. "I don't think I quite heard your name, *Fräulein*. Perhaps it was the momentary distractions of such beguiling gentlemanly company here," she said, aiming that in Moody's direction, causing him to look away in embarrassment. "I dare admit, it's a weakness of mine, delightful evening companions to wile away the hours. Pity it moves along so quickly when one isn't in a state of perpetual boredom. The need for company, companionship, having it here. It's often so . . . " She met Monty's gaze once again, her expression softening. " . . . *stimulating*."

The good doctor felt the tingling warmth of the word spread all the way up his spine to the base of his skull. He found himself utterly unable to look away, as if already frozen in place, turned to stone.

Clyde, however, wasn't falling under the young woman's spell. She'd encountered plenty of sirens in her life, and she'd discovered that all of them shared a common weakness, something that would often bring them back to the land of mere mortals, and that particular weakness was easily exploited. She managed a drawn, half-cooked smile as she stepped in between Monty and the young woman, blocking the view from both parties. All she wanted was a wash, a hot meal, and a bed, nothing more, and she'd make certain that would all happen for her, even if it meant she'd have to bathe in a trough and sleep with livestock for the night. Therefore, she'd get her introductions done and have their hosts moving in a less leisurely pace.

"Clyde Northway, soon to be Darrow," she said to the young woman. "And I don't think I heard your name, Miss . . . Do you prefer 'Miss'?"

That seemed to work, though not in the way Clyde had intended, for instead of answering her, the young woman smoothly moved away from Clyde, her demeanor instantly changing back to match the stiff formality of the older hosts with her back erect and her actions swift. The young woman snapped something in German to the Adlers. Mr. Adler then gave a curt head nod before taking some of the baggage the group had brought up the winding flight of stairs. On the other hand, Mrs. Adler had countered the young woman, her voice grating and shrill, and it wasn't long before the two of them were arguing, causing all sorts of uncomfortable confusion among their guests, all of whom exchanged uneasy glances at each other.

The guests broke away from one another, leaving the young woman and Mrs. Adler to their strange little tiff. Patience was still entranced by the décor of the house and wandered around, examining everything from the oil paintings that adorned the walls to the old grandfather clock in one corner that had suddenly chimed, announcing the passing of yet another evening hour. Moody attempted to take hold of Patience's bag, prying its handle from her husband's grip. Finch, red-faced and flustered with everything happening around him, shook Moody's grip off, offering an awkward grin as he did. He mouthed "I got it" to the kid, but Moody wasn't having it. He tried tugging the bag again from Finch, which inevitably led to a silent tug-of-war, both men insistent on taking the bags. It was finally Moody who won, and loaded with bags, he staggered up the staircase.

The good doctor and Clyde were still standing there, unsure of how to react with the Adler women who had reached the apex of their argument. Clyde removed her hat carefully from her updo, easing the pins back along with the stray strands that had escaped and danced in the wind earlier. Monty followed her lead and removed his own, instantly seeming to take off ten years from his age as he did. While Clyde normally wasn't one to marvel about such things about the men she encountered, she permitted herself to be momentarily distracted. His light brown hair was wavy and glossy, full of health and redolent of care even after having been trapped under his hat. He met her glance, his dark eyes smiling mischief at her.

Clyde was quick to look away, silently chastising herself for such frivolous flirtation. It wasn't as if she didn't appreciate being looked at, admired even. She often enjoyed the tingly rush of warmth in those moments. However, she simply couldn't afford to be anchored to idle pleasantries when there were . . . *complications* that would distract her from her duties.

And such duties were an absolute priority in her life as it was.

The young woman and Mrs. Adler finally ended

their row, with Mrs. Adler huffing away towards what looked to be a dining room to the other side of the stairwell. The young woman then turned back to the little group left there, looking around at each other, unsure of themselves. "Ladies, you will find you belongings in your room," she said in Patience and Clyde's direction. "It will be the second room on your right. The gentlemen will be in the room across the hall. Mr. Evers!" she called out to Moody, who had reached the landing, bags dangling from his grip, and was standing there, unsure of where to move. She then turned back to the travelers with a scoff and a wave. "Apologies in advance for lack of décor. It looks akin to a convent in all of its austerity."

Patience grabbed her husband's hand, pulling him back towards her as he was tripping over himself, gaping up at the wall hangings, the ornate fixtures, and the grand staircase. "I swear you're like a child, Finch Henry. Can't keep you near me without you wanderin', all wide-eyed at the finery."

She tugged him up the stairs with her, urging him on. Both Monty and Clyde stood at the base of the stairwell, looking awkwardly at each other. He gestured for her to go ahead of him up the stairs, and she did the same, insistence in her demeanor, teeth gritted. This went on for a good minute before their hostess' tinkling laugh broke their self-consciousness.

"Your fellow travelers didn't seem swayed by civility," she said as she moved in between them and up the stairs, beckoning them up with her. "Come. I'll take you on a tour of our grand estate and all its wonders."

So up the stairs they went just as the raindrops

pelted the windows, growing in tempo, and the grandfather clock announced the late afternoon had officially become the evening.

THREE

LEARTUS "CALL ME 'LEE' Goddamnit or Don't Call Me a Goddamn Thing" Shurchell wasn't the kind of man to engage in idle chatter over home-cooked meals on bone china followed by after-dinner brandy. He wasn't the sort to sleep indoors either, buried under a goose down comforter, snuggling with a pillow. He left that to the flush and fancy passengers. Their drivers like hell wouldn't have been permitted to sleep inside with the others. However, this new one, this Moody Evers fellow, he'd been treated like a whip, ace-high. Room and board, all the rest. Richer than possum gravy. But Lee knew there was something not quite right with the boy. For one, he was so goddamned loud, always jawing and chawing about the Lord, Our God and something about the bounty the Lord, Our God provided and how thankful they all ought to be over it.

Frankly, Lee couldn't give a cock spit over the Lord, Our God because the Lord, Our God hadn't done shit for Lee over the last few years when he'd given up his father's land due to his own accumulated debts. Granted, some of those "debts" were foolishly self-inflicted, which may or may not have included the occasional bottle . . . or two . . . or several more . . . of whiskey and the company of the voluptuous female sort for the night, but that was none of anyone's business but Lee's, thank you very goddamned much.

So Lee settled into a profession he'd naturally been comfortable with, one that involved deliveries and protection. He was good at protecting anything that wasn't his own, especially when that particular protection involved some action. Action by way of gunslinging and lightening quick reflexes, of course. Once, he'd been lucky enough to defend a Wells Fargo stage from a fusillade courtesy of the notorious McCarty Gang. Along with the resourceful whip and Rusty, the other guard, Lee had set up an ambush of his own, taking back their supplies and the stage's express packages after a hail of gunfire. Thankfully then, only one of the McCarty boys was injured, a skim just at the curve of his right ear, making the kid easy to identify for the authorities and earning Lee some high praise from his contemporaries (namely, his drinking-and-whoring buddies from way back when). Yep, that was back when shootouts were a thing and a man was worth his weight in ammunition.

Ever since the train route expansions though, those goddamned locomotives, Lee was lucky to even get work on the outskirts, providing transport between the rural communities that weren't within reasonable distance to a station. He supposed he could count his blessings, and all that godly horseshit the Evers boy wouldn't shut up about, but Lee didn't presume he'd be entirely unable to find a good day's— hell, a good week's worth of work, not while westward expansion was no longer a mere dream of men. Out there in the wide, vast open, men could be free, away from the dark clouds that hovered over the urbanites and lingered with storm over the already-forgotten soldiers of the East. Lee may have had his troubles, but he was only reminded of them on days when he'd had to converse with anybody, even those who were worthwhile of his time. When he was alone with the rolling land, his true love, all was as it should be.

Right then though, Lee was on edge. When he'd tended to the horses in the stables, he'd run into the hostler, one of the Adler kin, the eldest child he presumed. Although "child" was a word that didn't exactly spring to mind when Lee turned right into him. He couldn't have been but seventeen at most, but Lee had first thought he'd run into a beast of an actual man. The "boy" towered well over six feet five inches (Lee was five eleven, so the kid just *loomed* over him). His body was all muscle and granite, his girth as solid around as an ox. When Lee tipped back his bowler to get a good look at his face, he was greeted with a steely hardness that belied the boy's age. It was as if the kid had stepped into a rocky adulthood and had then decided to set up camp there for the rest of his days. He also looked as if he'd seen something odd he couldn't connect with, his low brow in a deep, permanent furrow. His red-rimmed eyes stared blankly at Lee, and the boy just stood there in front of him, almost as if he were challenging Lee to push.

"Don't you worry none. I'll make sure they're fed n'watered, an' I'll be out here with them tonight," Lee said, looking the manchild straight in the eye as he did. Lee had long learned after having survived plenty of punches from his pa that it was always best to look a man in the eye to show dominance and authority. (Mainly, it was just to show that Lee wasn't about to take any goddamned shit from a kid.) But the manchild didn't move from his spot. Instead, he just continued to stare down at Lee with those empty bloodshot eyes.

Lee stepped back to give the kid a long up-down, his head cocked at him. "Boy, you speak even a lick of English?"

He then leaned in, his hand slowly snaking down to his holster where he'd kept his baby, his Smith and Wesson Model 3 given to him by a passenger whose little girl he'd put together a cozy, makeshift shelter for during a particularly nasty storm. The girl's father had been so grateful; he'd felt it only natural to thank him, man-to-man, with the finest firearm Lee had ever seen. His baby had then saved him on more than one occasion when the ride got rough and the saloon brawls got heated, which was often the case whenever Lee was around—the curse of a man who just looked as if he was primed and ticking for a fight no matter where he was in the world.

The curse of a man who lived and died again and again in a land gone mad with dour stakes and constant greed.

"Son, I strongly advise you turn tail an' allow a man some solitude here," Lee continued, keeping that edge in his tone. He was goddamned sure to make the manchild understand who was actually bossman and who was there to serve. "Ain't you got a barnyard in which you can roam? Got some pigs to feed? Cattle to herd along? Sheep to fuck? I ain't one to engage in jibber-jabber. Spent the past dawn 'til dusk, attemptin' to ignore that lil turd beside me and his biblical horseshit, on and on, an' I ain't in the mood for more. Just want some quiet s'all." He waited for the giant to speak, to respond in any way at all, but the manchild simply turned around and tromped out of the stables.

Since the manchild had left him to his thoughts, Lee had fed the horses, stroking their whuffling muzzles, murmuring gentle words, as he moved from one stall to the next, watching them as they munched and grunted. It was the last truly loving gesture he could offer as a man of the land, the only one that mattered there. He also didn't really mind the chatter, as long as it was on his terms. Horses seemed to talk back in their way when they were either elated or afraid, and Lee had learned over the years of living out in the wide open that when they trusted a man, their bond was as good as any human's, sometimes better.

The Evers boy had quickly grown acclimated to Lee's need for solitude, and the two of them had fallen into a routine over the short amount of time they'd worked together, and that worked well for Lee. He'd absolutely no interest in educating stage drivers repetitiously about his own ways. The younger the driver, he'd found, the less trouble since all they wanted to do was do "right" as Evers had sagely remarked during a particular conversation that Lee, for once, hadn't minded a bit.

Lee had then unraveled his bedroll and spread out the sougan on a bare patch of floor in the only empty stall in the stables. It had been a long day's journey, and a man wasn't much of a thinking, cautious man if he neglected to care for himself, and that care included just enough rest even if it was a mite early in the evening. Lee kept his sole possessions bundled in a gunnysack, tucked in a hard knot behind his head. His pistol was still holstered since a man was barely any good without it at night. Additionally, Lee was such a light sleeper, it wouldn't take much jostling around to wake him should a fool feel the urge to rob him of his most prized possession. Like a goddamned thieving hand would come away with anything but broken fingers. There were times when Lee wished some idiot would try, just to see how quickly he could snap 'em all, rendering the sonofabitch's shooting hand useless.

That was the last thought running through his head, stretching a smile across Lee's sun-creased, rawhide face. He'd barely drifted off when he suddenly snapped awake, fully alert, his hand grappling for his holstered weapon. Lee's breathing came in shallow, steady gasps, so he shut his mouth tightly, exhaling through his nostrils.

The last time he'd woken with such a start had been months ago, and he'd put a bullet in a prostitute's skull. That firebrand of a filly, a redhead by the name of Lizette, had woken him up with the jingling sound of her rummaging around his belongings, the coins pinging from their hiding spot. As soon as she'd heard the click of the hammer being cocked, Lizette had turned around slowly, a coquettish smile breaking out like sunshine across her rosy face. She playfully raised her hands in mock surrender at him, smirking at the gun he'd aimed at her. The coin sack slipped from her nimble fingers followed by the muffled, tinkling plop of the sack hitting the wood floor.

With cat-like movements, she'd slid down on the bed, moving stealthily towards Lee. He'd kept the pistol trained on her, his cold gaze steady. Lizette giggled and pouted at Lee, teasing him as she crawled over his legs. He stared at her as she licked the barrel as if it were a prick, taking her time with her tongue, sliding it towards him, then back, in towards him, then back. She'd then taken the muzzle in between her lips and sucked it noisily, engulfing it whole, her eyes flirting embers at him as she fellated his weapon.

Lee hadn't much cared for her little display. Frankly, he'd found the whole thing goddamned repugnant. So, naturally, he'd pulled the trigger, sending the back of Lizette's head splattering chunks of brains and skull fragments against the floral-patterned wall, giving it a nice crimson touch. Lee had then yanked the muzzle from Lizette's bloody maw, her limp, marionette body jerking forward, back, and then slumping face-first on the bedspread.

Needless to say, it didn't matter a goddamned bit to the madam. He'd paid her handsomely, pardoning the mess he'd left behind, and she'd not even blinked at the sight of Lizette's prone form, the back of her head having virtually disintegrated, and the gore-spattered wall. Instead, the madam had stuffed the coin sack down her ample bosom and nodded him off, a signal for him to leave and do so without any sort of wayward objection, which Lee, of course, was more than willing to do. Hell, it was the least he could do.

Granted, he'd lost a fair bit of coin, that moment

forever etched in rue, but since then, he'd been goddamned sure he was never alone with a feisty whore with the kind of confidence that often ended with a man drinking himself to the bottom of yet another bottle of despair.

That, and he'd always remained alert, gun at the ready, even when on the welcome cusp of slumber.

The storm outside had turned violent and cruel, the wind and rain lashing at the rickety foundation of the stable. Lee wasn't right sure if it had been the shrieking winds happening out there that had jolted him awake like that or if it had been something coming from someplace inside the stable, something there with him and the whinnying horses in the dark. He sat up and slid backwards until his back tapped against the wall of the stall where he'd lain for the night. His pistol was already out, cocked, and ready as he sat there and listened.

Just listened there in the dark.

Listened for the slightest variation in sound, over the stormy din.

A crack of thunder shook Lee, tearing him out of his concentration. His pistol hand, still aiming at the shadow play in front of him, trembled slightly. He tightened his grip and silently cursed himself for his momentary scare. Lee had never been rattled before, but that edge had snuck up on him ever since he'd caught sight of the Adler house looming there from across the plains.

That goddamned house.

Wasn't right. Something off about it. The whole place. It felt like it belonged elsewhere. Some landscape in dreams concocted by wealthy fuckbirds who'd gotten their wings and traveled the world before they'd decided to build on land they'd known nothing about. Not as if they'd cared either. That sort of aloof carelessness was always evident in their architecture. Nothing ever seemed to be practical, but it wasn't as if they'd given a good goddamn about that, not even.

The place, at the very least, was made to weather storms, its foundation solid. Hell, even through all its creaks and groans, the stable seemed a part of the earth, not giving in without a fight.

It wasn't the weather conditions out there that had woken Lee though. He knew, somehow, he wasn't alone with the horses.

"Why don't you come out an' show your ugly face," Lee called out in the dark. "Ain't gonna shoot you if you make yourself known. You step right in front of me n' stay there, an' I'll put my girl away, nice and neat, so she won't get temperamental."

Lee kept the pistol trained on the space in front of him, his mouth curling into a clenched sneer. His teeth ground together, but he kept quiet, careful about listening for those slight deviations in sound that betrayed the fool who was attempting to stay hidden in the darkness. He waited patiently, letting the minutes pass on by. He was used to waiting. There'd been many nights he'd kept his eyes open, body alert, easing his breathing as he watched over his passengers and driver after they'd settled into slumber for the night. He'd trained himself to actively listen and control his own sounds, like he was nothing more than a shadow, blending with the darkness around him.

When nothing emerged from the pitch, no sign of anything at all, Lee settled back down on the sougan his heart still thudding in his ears. It was the one thing he couldn't control, and it had often given him such trouble during those quiet nights when he was on high alert. If drink didn't kill him, it would sure as hell be his heart that sometimes couldn't take the strain of his secret: that he was little more than cold stew on the inside; thus, it wouldn't take much to make him shit his pants. He couldn't have it that way, not when he had a certain reputation to hold onto, and it was that sort of reputation that would all but guarantee a man his claim in history. (Or so his father, the old sot, had lectured him time and time again, more often after he'd caned Lee's hide to shreds for something goddamned stupid.)

Lee shut his eyes, attempting to ready himself for slumber once more, images of a previous life, a boy's world with fishing, horse-playing, and pain, so much pain, scrolling through his mind. Fuck if that sort of thing didn't make a man weep like a baby. His eyes grew filmy with hot tears, and as he wiped them clean away, he heard the ever so slight shuffling sound of someone, or something, moving in the dark. He drew his arm away, and the blurry mountain was standing right there, looming over him.

Before Lee could reach for his gun, the mountain lifted its leg and its heavy, boot-clad foot stomped his face with such force, Lee's nose was instantly reduced to mush, bits of bone and cartilage cracking inward upon impact. His face, a mask of blood and gristle, burned, his screams muffled by blood and snot. His teeth were mashed from his upper jaw, lodging in his throat, making it near impossible to inhale that much needed air.

Lee's hand flailed at his side, fingers clawing for his weapon, but then the mountainous mass above drove down the prong end of a pitchfork, sending its tines into his forearm, sending searing pain up his shoulder. The tines pinned his arm to the wooden floor of the stall, preventing him from moving it.

Blood filled Lee's mouth and it trickled from his flattened nose to his eyes, blinding him further, which, in all goddamned retrospect, was probably a blessing. After all, he didn't need to see the killing blow, that boot coming down again and mashing his head to the consistency of jelly that matched his coward's innards. Lee's face disintegrated upon impact, caving in on itself. The giant, the Adler manchild, ground his foot into what remained of Lee's head, twisting it back and forth, robbing the corpse of any resemblance of the man it had been.

When the manchild lifted his foot from the shattered remains of Lee's head, stringy clots of bloody goo clung to the sole of his boot, connecting the boot to the meaty mess it had created. He let out a low squeal of disgust, as if it had been the absolute worst thing about the whole ordeal. He didn't like the thought of anything left behind, anything dirty . . . anything *filthy*. He'd taken such care of his boots before. He didn't mind if they'd been scuffed. He just couldn't stand shit and gore touching his clothes, or at least touching the things he'd taken pride in. He knew he wasn't handsome. His *Mutter* had reminded him daily of that fact. At the very least, he could keep himself tidy, and *sauberkeit ist frömmigkeit,* as his mother had said to him again and again.

Cleanliness *is* godliness. An absolute truth.

He would let the rain rid his boots of the mess from the shotgun's head. He would have to. His *Mutter* would not have it otherwise, and he'd spend another night sleeping alone, an embarrassment, away from the big house. On nights when he was tidy and meticulous, he'd been permitted to sleep in the carriage house, mere steps from the big house. A night in the big house was his dream. Those beds with their plump goose down bedding and colorful quilts. The smoky, heady smells of crackling fire in the fireplace and roasting guinea fowl coupled by the soft aroma of rose petals that followed *her* wherever she went.

Her. Just the thought of being in the same domain as *her* made his heart flutter, his breath catch in his throat, his groin tingle. His *Mutter* had promised him many times over that one day, he would be rewarded, that he would have *her* in the big house, in a real bed, to do with what he pleased. He would finally be able to glide his fingers over that ivory smooth skin and lick each and every precious inch of her. He would worship her flesh, finally tasting what *Gott* crafted Himself from the rib with His own hands. He would then bury his fat cock deep within her, impaling her with it, before filling her with his seed. They would create more life to please *Mutter.*

After all, Family is wealth; Family is life. *Familie ist alles.*

Until that day when he would be allowed in the big house to be with *her*, he would have to satisfy himself. There was no point in delaying his pleasure, saving it all for *her*. Once again, he assuaged his desperate physical need by unbuttoning his trousers, pulling out his cock, and then frantically jerking at its foreskin until he could no longer stand it. His whole body shuddered as he climaxed in jerking spurts over the mushed head of the shotgun, his spunk mingling with the chunky red stew of what was left of the shotgun's face.

As he often did after he came, and after he'd tucked his damp, wilting cock away, he leaned against whatever post or wall was there, panting, his eyes wet from the exertion. The last, lingering image that ran through his head, searing his brain, was that of his *Mutter* on fire, screaming for him to die with her. He never understood why that was what it was, why that particular vision. He often thought it was an omen.

If that was the case, why did he often feel his cock coming to life once again, throbbing in his trousers? And once again, he'd have the need.

Quite often, as he learned through routine, it was a signal for the real events of the evening to begin.

FOUR

CLYDE NORTHWAY DIDN'T care much
for frivolity, especially in the littlest of things
that owned a woman rather than vice versa.

One would garner this little fact about Clyde if
they were so inclined to search through her
belongings. Only a snoop would, mind you, and the
Adler girl, the younger one with the scar that mashed
one corner of her lips together, had perfected the art
of the silent snoop and not simply due to the fact she
didn't speak. The girl put her ear to the wall that
divided the lone, empty room at the end of the upper
floor corridor to the guest room that had always been
bequeathed to the lady travelers. When she heard the
tiny squeak of unoiled metal hinged to metal, the
scarred girl peeked through the hole there in the wall,
one she'd discovered when the family had moved in.
She'd covered it with a wall hanging, a faded quilt
she'd found in a cedar-lined trunk in the attic. It was
the only décor, the only bright spot in a room that was
shrouded in filtered grey emptiness.

In the ladies' guest room, Patience was washing
herself down in the copper tub that had been set near
the fireplace. She dipped a washrag in the rose
scented water and scrubbed at her arms, her armpits,

the back of her neck, over and under each of her heavy breasts, singing softly as she did. She stopped what she was doing, wringing out the cloth over her chest just before she unraveled and hung it over the rim of the tub. Then she slid in the tub, dangled her legs over the rim as she dipped back, splashing water onto the floor as she did. The girl couldn't fully see what Patience was doing, but it wasn't hard to assume she'd submerged herself in the water enough so she'd sloshed much of it out of the tub to the floor.

Beside the bed the ladies were to share, Clyde was in the process of dressing again, having washed beforehand. She buttoned her dress jacket once more. Then, with her back to Patience, Clyde had taken a roll of raggedy cloth from her carpet bag and unraveled it carefully over the bedspread. She put on a thick leather arm brace, what looked almost like a long, fingerless glove bulky with a strange weight against her dorsal forearm. Upon closer inspection from where she peeked, the scarred girl caught glimpses of thin straps, like rings, looped around Clyde's index and ring fingers, both straps connected to the brace. She couldn't tell much from her spot. She also couldn't see what Clyde had unraveled from the cloth and had, by then, spread out on the bed as well. From what the girl could tell, Clyde had stiffened her stance as she examined the cloth's contents, and before she could pick up what she was looking at, there was a sharp rap at the door, startling both Clyde and the scarred girl.

Patience suddenly heaved herself up in the tub. She spat out water and pushed the tangled weave of wet hair from her eyes.

"What is it now?" snapped Clyde, and before the scarred girl could discern any of what Clyde had laid out, Clyde had quickly covered the contents of her bag with one of the blankets that had been folded neatly on the bed prior.

"Finch Henry, you'd best be mindin' yer own," called out Patience in the direction of the door. "We're not suitable, hear?"

Monty laughed from the other side of the door, his mellow chuckle muffled. "Forgive me, ladies. I certainly didn't mean to interrupt your toilet," he said. "I was sent to inform you that supper is being served."

Patience giggled into a palm and then twisted herself around in the tub to steal a glance in the direction of her roommate. Clyde still had her back to the tub, but the scarred girl had her in full view, and she saw the tightened jaw, the exasperated eye roll just before Clyde made her way over to the door. Before she opened the door, she stood there for a moment in deep contemplation. Her gaze was far-reaching, traveling further to the thoughts that seemed to drift from her, and then she turned her head and looked straight ahead at the wall, directly at the hole where the scarred girl spied from, the hole that was meant to blend in with the dark patterned wallpaper.

The girl gasped, pulling back, her hand over her mouth. The blood coursed in her ears, her nerves rattled. She didn't think Clyde had seen anything, but she couldn't be certain. There was something about the lady that unnerved her. It wasn't the strange accessories or adornments she had brought with her. It was the way she held herself, as if she was braced for something to happen and the way she seemed to carefully be observing everything around her.

That one, the girl thought, *that one might very well spell trouble for the household.*

Not that the girl cared in the slightest. It was high time for things to take a turn.

And maybe, just maybe, the fancy woman with the strange attire could improve on matters in the house. She looked the type.

Lord knew the house could use the type.

The good doctor stood patiently outside the door, a slight dance of a smile playing on the corner of his lips. He'd stepped back from the door in the dimly lit hall. After all, a gentleman would never listen in on conversations that were none of his affair, and the to-be Mrs. Darrow and young Mrs. Wilkson, as vastly differing in mannerisms as they were, were still the ladies of the house, and what sort of words they exchanged during their evening preparations were not for prying men's ears. Monty wouldn't dare to presume he'd been bequeathed an invitation to join them in their chatter.

When the door to the ladies' guest room finally opened, a cloud of sweet-smelling rose and talcum powder surrounded Monty in a soft tangle of an embrace as her silhouette came into view. Clyde was breathless, her skin flushed, as if he'd just caught her in the middle of something she shouldn't have been doing. From what he'd ascertained over the events of the day and from what he'd observed of her, he knew full well she was hiding something significant.

He didn't expect it would be polite of him to attempt to find out what it was about her that had his nerves jangled whenever she was near.

Even still, it could be a delightful bit of fun.

"Pardon my intrusion," Monty said, clearing his throat, a blush heating his face, the back of his neck, the warmth of it trickling down his spine. "I—I certainly didn't mean to interrupt you ladies, but as I said before—"

"You were sent," said Clyde, her mouth settling into a wry smile. "Yes, you've said as much."

"I was also told to relay that supper would be difficult to keep on the table as the . . . Oh, how did our lovely hostess state it . . . Yes . . . 'The gentlemen travelers and the layabouts of the house' would be taken by their appetites, so there would be naught but empty platters and full bellies by the time those charming ladies graced us with their presence."

Clyde cocked an eyebrow at him. "Did she now?"

"In all honesty, I added the 'charming' bit."

"That *did* sound like you."

That brought up the crinkles around his eyes as his smile widened. The woman and her biting wit. "Was it too much?" he said, feigning concern. "Perhaps I should've kept it sardonic? Something more suited to your person?"

It was Clyde's turn to give back a half-cocked, wry grin as she leaned against the door. "Suited to my 'person'? Why, whatever are you implying, doctor? What would 'sardonic' entail?"

He cleared his throat again, and she chuckled at his embarrassment. His little foible she'd enjoyed. "What I meant to—I didn't mean to seem coarse, Miss

Northway. You don't strike me as a woman of the afternoon tea variety. Not inclined to partake in frivolous natter when there are matters of importance."

"So women are more often of the 'afternoon tea variety'? And I'm not particularly . . . *womanly*. Is that what you're saying?"

He leaned ever so slightly in towards her, his eyes daring her own to play. "It sounds as if you know precisely what I mean by that."

Clyde took it one step further, pushing her back away from the door, her face inches from his own. Her gaze trailed from his eyes to his full lips, his rich beard. He smelled of sweet tobacco and whiskey, a bit of wood smoke, that hint of the autumn months on the edge there. She let out a long sigh, a deliberate move, a slight whisper of breath to tease at his lips. Monty swallowed back his nerves, his eyes locked on hers.

"Ah, but would you know what was 'womanly,' even if you sensed it there, even if you *touched* it," she purred, her mouth close, so very close, to brushing against his. "Would you now, doctor?"

"Mrs. Darrow—"

"Am I no longer Miss Northway?"

The good doctor stepped back from her, his stance growing firm and steady once again, all business. "Forgive me, but I consider myself a gentleman, and I don't think it would behoove me to assume a lady of your standing would—"

Clyde laughed, sharp titter of noise, and clamped her hand over her mouth, her eyes dancing in merriment at Monty, who looked utterly taken aback at her laughter. "Oh, I'm teasing, you, doctor!" she said around a chortle. "Look at you now, all befuddled there, all pink-cheeked and suddenly such a boy. Such a *boy* at heart, aren't you?"

"Dr. Pickering, sir?" Moody shouted from the base of the stairs.

"What's that, Mr. Evers?" the good doctor called out, relieved for once for the momentary diversion. His evasiveness towards her in the moment was something Clyde further warmed to as she leaned back against the door, watching him closely.

"Lady of the house don't want you idlin' for so long up there, sir! Says this is a godly house, not a den of sin an' temptation!"

Clyde made a face at Monty, crossing her eyes at him in mock exasperation. He caught her just at that instance and couldn't contain his chuckle.

"In other words, she don't want you jawin', makin' a mash with the lady travelers none! Just make sure the doctor comes back downstairs an' such s'what she said!"

"'Jawin' and makin' a mash'," whispered Clyde, punctuating it with a wry smirk.

Monty held up a finger at her, at which she shook her head, before he answered, "Kindly inform the lady of the house that I've done my duty here and will be joining the men in a moment!"

"Well n' good, sir! I'll pass that on for ya!"

"The men need to partake in their evening whiskeys and tobacco," Clyde said. "Keep them well away from the delicate women tending to their ladybusiness. What do you suppose that ladybusiness is all about, doctor? So mysterious."

57

"I wouldn't presume to know, Miss Northway," he said. "Frankly, I think there are some things best left silent, especially those sorts of dark thoughts of terrible men with terrible hearts."

The two of them stood there for a moment, awkward in their silence for once.

It was Clyde who broke the stillness, her gaze diverted to something past the good doctor's shoulder. She stepped around him, her face furrowed. Curious, Monty turned to see what she was suddenly fixated on. It was a peculiar ferrotype in a plain wooden frame hanging on the wall of the hallway.

He craned to get a closer look at it. In the image, there was a tight, little group of men and women and a little boy, who was gaping, wide-eyed at the photographer. They had all clustered in front of the stairs leading up to the very same, grand house Clyde and Monty were standing in.

Clyde's attention solely fixated on the center of the image. A bunched frown lined her pale face, forming grooves in her brow and to the sides of her mouth. Monty glanced at her and then at what was holding her attention.

She sensed him there, searching for whatever it was she was staring at, so, using the tip of her pinkie, she lightly traced the shape of one of the women in the image. She was standing on the top step behind a stout, angry faced, middle-aged woman. Both women were dressed alike in simple, high-necked, black frocks, but the one Clyde was fixated on was the stout woman's opposite in manner and appearance. She was slender in stature with wispy light-colored tresses on top of her head.

Her youthful face, while serious in expression, seemed to hold the brightness of the sun at its center. She had life in her eyes, a touch of something, amusement perhaps, as they focused on the photographer.

"She's quite fetching," murmured the doctor. "Mother and daughter, perhaps? Aunt and niece? Sisters? Although, they seem to have a significant age difference. Perhaps if they'd been—"

Clyde let her hand drop to her side, her eyes still fixated on the ferrotype. "Governess and ward," she said simply.

Monty turned to her, startled. "You know this how?"

"It doesn't matter."

"But if they'd traveled the same route and had stopped here—"

She looked at him. Her expression, flat, unreadable. "As I've said, it doesn't *matter*."

"Miss Northway," he said softly. "We're fellow travelers here, all sharing the same sort of concerns among strangers. It would behoove us to assume some sort of . . . *trust* between us since we're locked here for the night."

"Trust must be earned, Doctor Pickering," she bit back. "And you are still quite far from having earned the slightest bit from me."

"Fair enough." He was then quiet, contemplating her words before clearing his throat and asking, "Do you recognize them?"

Clyde's gaze drifted back to the picture. She seemed as if she'd been about to say something, but whatever it was had caught in her throat. She was in another place, standing there, and the doctor was unsure as to how to bring her back.

So he touched her arm, his fingertips barely brushing the strange solidity of the brace she had attached there. Clyde broke from her thoughts and jerked her arm away, glaring at him and drawing her arm in towards her chest. She backed away from him, her face masked with a grimace. Monty realized he'd broken any chance he might have had at gaining her trust.

It was whatever she had strapped around her arm. It must have been. The fact she'd gone from confident and assured to so suddenly self-conscious and suspicious from the slightest touch. He held up his hands in apology.

"I shouldn't have. Forgive me."

But Clyde was already facing the door, her hand on the doorknob, twisting it.

"Miss Northway, it's apparent that I've overstepped boundaries. However, if you are in need of a professional opinion on treatment for an injured arm—"

"Treatment for an *injured* arm," she muttered through clenched teeth as she opened the door.

"—I may certainly be of assistance as my particular area of expertise lies in—"

The door slammed in the good doctor's face.

"Miss Northway, our hosts await!" he called out. "It would be rude not to . . . Oh . . . " Monty's voice dropped in embarrassment. "Well, that was productive, wasn't it, you halfwit?" he mumbled. "Ever so nicely done, old man."

He turned away from the bedroom door and

found himself looking straight at the picture once again, its strange pull now enhanced by the backstory it apparently shared with the lady in the red dress.

Of all people.

FIVE

MUTTI HAD PROMISED good things come to good girls who wait, good girls who are patient and careful and bide their time, good girls who, while charming and gracious to their guests, understood their place in the world as it was.

Such good things.

Things like silk dresses and delicate china, handsome gentlemen callers and dancing. Oh, to dream of *dancing*. There would be blooming flower gardens and card-playing in the parlor until the early hours. Brandy and music. Amusing patter, chiming laughter. Perhaps even a leisurely stroll, arm-in-arm with someone tall and divine, whose eyes twinkled in amusement, diamonds in the dark.

Someone even like *Doktor* Pickering. A girl could get lost in the fantasy. He was *herrlich*, a spark of life in the prairie. She just didn't belong out there. Neither did *der Doktor*. The two of them, they belonged in the city where life blossomed, where women could be properly cared for. None of the drudgery. None of the tedious work outdoors that turned girls into bone husks with sun-roughened skin and little humor, so little life in their empty eyes.

Work that changed girls into . . . *Männer*.

Mutti had been that sort of woman forever it seemed. She never laughed, but she never cried either. The land had hardened her to stone. *Vati* had seen to that with his demands of her, of his family. The only sense of excitement anyone could get out of *Mutti* was the prospect of travelers. After all, travelers were their livelihood in their current state. It had been that way for several years come winter.

Travelers also meant never growing too comfortable where one lay, always being alert, ready for anything to happen at any time.

She had been pleased that, for once, they had all followed her advice from the very beginning of their journey into the vast land, the new spaces and possibilities, and had treated her with the sort of reverence and respect usually reserved for the true toilers of the land. The men, in other words. They all listened when she instructed them to do something, her words edged with truths they could not deny anymore. She had been *richtig* throughout the months.

Eventually, that sort of respect would give her some sense of leadership among them. She would be *ready* when it finally happened.

But first, wit and charm were the orders of the evening. She had taught them all the correct positioning coupled with respectable social norms, *sitten und bräuche* above all. They would appear gracious and kind to their guests, those travelers, all the way to the guests' end of their journey.

The table had been beautifully set with the china that had been brought out specially from the dining room's sideboard. *Mutti* had supplemented the dish with crusty bread and a hearty stew redolent of rich, salt pork fat and thick with beef and root vegetables.

That particular meal, purposefully heavy and enough for an army, was often *Mutti's* signal to all of them that she was wary, that someone among the travelers would be difficult. That they were to be cautious, ready for a long night ahead. A well-fed guest would be sluggish, *schleppend*, unable to concentrate and move quickly and carefully.

Which traveler did *Mutti* suppose would be difficult?

It would make for an interesting evening, like a guessing game where only a secret, select few would be competitors. No matter, *Mutti* would want each and every one of them to watch their guests carefully for signs of danger. Some of the others over the years had engaged them in such terrible fights, enough to put *Vati* on bedrest for weeks.

They were good lessons in vigilance.

She supposed she would be ready when things grew . . . untidy.

And afterwards, well, good things come to *gute Mädchen* who wait, good girls who have patience.

In the meantime, there was a delicious meal ready for them.

Clyde didn't care for the pretense.

Still, she understood her station and accepted it as such. She could be charming, a delightful conversationalist, when the evening hours called for it. As that particular evening trudged along, she half-listened, half-responded in murmurs to the men and women at the supper table, while taking small bites of stew. The doctor was enamored as ever by the odd charms of the young Adler woman, who had especially intrigued his fancy with her talk of the metaphysical. She enthralled him with the claim that she could "read his aura" just by staring into his soul by way of his eyes. Absurd, of course, but while the two were so intent on the other, Clyde could quietly observe the rest of the supper party.

Her primary focus was on their hosts, especially the mother, who had been watching Clyde silently, her eyes narrowed and her mouth drawn in a crooked line. She had been about to bite into a piece of bread when the mother cleared her throat with a rattling cough, the sudden noise startling Clyde enough that she dropped the bread on her plate and locked eyes with the woman. She offered the mother what she'd hoped would come across as a friendly smile, but such women, Clyde understood, weren't particularly swayed by other women's attempts at charm. This was a woman who saw things as they were behind masks.

This was a woman who blatantly didn't care for Clyde.

Clyde's arm with the heavy brace had been tucked under the table, her hand curled in her lap. She was careful not to stretch her fingers, so she gritted through the prickling sensation happening in her hand. She'd bide her time with it. Timing was essential.

"It seems *Fraulein* Northway has left her appetite on the plains, *ja?*" Mr. Adler said with a gruff chortle, breaking the uncomfortably stiff silence between the two women. "You must eat more than that. Grow fat-bellied and happy so that you may sleep well tonight. My wife and our lovely Kate enjoy cooking for guests. They would be insulted if you did not eat everything on your plate."

Clyde turned her focus on their host and watched as he sopped up the dregs of stew left on his plate with his hunk of bread. He popped the bread in his mouth, and beefy dribble ran down from the corner of his mouth to his wooly beard where it was promptly lost in the wiry mass. He patted down his beard with a napkin, his eyes glinting back at Clyde as he did.

She didn't like the way his dark eyes went strangely glassy when he stared, like he was looking past her rather than at her. She had observed over the years that his was a look certain men had when they were contemplating something ghastly.

"Well, it was ab-so-*lutely* delicious, Mrs. and *Miss* Adler," Monty said, breaking the awkward silence between their host and Clyde as he wiped down his mouth and mustache with his napkin. "A welcome respite after a day's journey with nothing substantial other than dried provisions."

"I agree, ma'am," Finch chimed in. "Them 'dried provisions' don't do much but keep you alert and moderately sated. You cain't get grub as fine a spread as this here, not out in wild country. I 'specially thought the potato dumplin's as tasty as my granny used to make. And she never once shared her recipe with anyone. Here's hopin' my Patience here'll be charmin' plenty enough to get it outta Granny someday."

Patience snickered and said, "Finch Henry, you know your granny don't care for me none. Be lucky if I can get that woman's ear at all, what with her hearin' goin' southways. Whenever anyone talks to her, they got to shout, which she don't like if you're a proper lady anyway. Tell me how'm I supposed to get that woman's attention if she don't want me shoutin' none?"

"She likes you plenty, honey. Didn't she show you her bone china she done brought all the way from the old country? She loves her china."

"Yeah, only to tell me not to go near any of it 'cause she said she thought I was some kinda 'clumsy heifer' and might break it all."

The pretty Adler hostess, Kate, laughed around the rim of her wine glass, took a dainty sip from it, and then set it down beside her plate, which, Clyde noted, was still loaded with food. It was the same with Mrs. Adler's dish. Mr. Adler had wolfed down his serving of the stew but hadn't even touched any of the potatoes and dumplings. Almost as if—

"So please . . . indulge us, the soon-to-be-Mrs. Darrow," Kate said, interrupting Clyde's thoughts. "Why here, of all places? This land is vast and empty, aside from some tribes out in the plains. It's deadlands, hardly adequate to settle."

"I'm sorry, I thought my pending marriage to the Commodore was perfectly clear. What piques your curiosity about it, Miss Adler?" She silently noted that other possibility, another warning sign, and stored it safely away in the recesses of her thoughts.

"You seem a lady of the city rather than one of the plains," Kate said. "One who enjoys tea from polished silver. High society. You're refined, evidently well-read, and your dress seems out of a Parisian catalogue. Are you willing to shed the finery for a laborious way of life? Again, why here? Why would you give all of that up to marry a wayward ex-military madman?"

"Kate, manners, *bitte*," growled Mr. Adler who then smiled broadly at Clyde. "Forgive our Kate. She is filled with curiosity, and she questions guests until they cannot take a breath."

"Oh, it's perfectly reasonable to ask this of me. After all, I'm not a woman of the plains. And the dress *is* from Paris, Miss Adler. You've a sharp eye and are certainly a woman of taste yourself. You dress as if you've been waiting for the right guests to arrive. Guests who would appreciate stylish women and their lavish homes. This place, it's grand. So surprising, for plains settlers, don't you think? Not normally what one comes to expect from a home station, those sad, little, squat sod houses." Clyde directed that squarely at Monty, whose attention kept fluctuating between the two women.

He nodded his agreement, swallowing down the bite of food that had been turning to mush in his mouth. Monty had been too enrapt in the conversation to focus on his meal, the conversation was bordering on a tiff between the ladies at the table.

Clyde could indulge in the young woman's game with no trouble at all. She enjoyed it for what it was worth. There was a type of personality Clyde had encountered during her time growing up in the city, one that required ever-vigilance and patience.

And constant, meticulous observation.

Before one could strike.

It was Mrs. Adler who finally spoke, breaking the hard silence among them. "This is our home, *Fraulein*. You are a guest here. It is impolite to remark . . . to question our means." She turned to her husband. "'Means'? *Ist das korrekt?*"

Mr. Adler chuckled. "*Ja. Ist gud.*" He looked at Clyde, his eyes sparkling with some semblance of life for once. "My wife does not understand . . . um . . . hypocrisy. It is *hypocritical* of her to disapprove of your curiosity with the same lack of manners she insists you have yourself. You do not have to respond."

Monty leaned over, about to pipe in, but Clyde held up her hand at him, signaling him to stop. "It's perfectly fine," she said and offered a friendly smile in Kate's direction. "It *was* rude of me to pry. You've been lovely hosts, and I apologize for my effrontery. I never once intended offense."

Kate returned the smile with a coy half-one, something she'd practiced in front of a mirror, Clyde surmised, as it looked forced, as if she was trying it on especially for a woman and didn't care for how it felt.

"So then, Miss Northway, would you mind awfully if you indulged me with my own inquiry as to why you *chose* to reside in the plains? You're a rarity out here, after all. A rose garden in the middle of the prairie. Not exactly a part of the natural landscape. Like something out of a delightful dream."

Clyde's cheeks and neck burned as she felt the heat of everyone's stare on her. Still, she supposed it was time for their hosts to be put in their place with a solitary warning shot, one that would either slow them down or backfire completely. She hoped it would be the former. Timing was crucial. She'd need all the time she could get. "Why am I here, out in the prairie? It's a good question, if a bit difficult to answer so simply, even effectively, I'd wager," Clyde mused. She then turned to her host who had set down his fork for once and had his full attention on her, as everyone else had.

"*Ich existiere, um den Westen zu zahmen,*" Clyde said.

The entirety of the table went silent. Finch, Patience, and Moody exchanged puzzled looks. Monty, however, couldn't contain his delight. His smile formed into a boyish grin, like he'd always known. The Adlers though, appeared shocked. Mrs. Adler's apple-rosy complexion had gone grey. Mr. Adler's face bunched into a scowl.

But it was Kate who broke the stillness with a tinkling laugh, and she clapped her hands, politely applauding in Clyde's direction. "Bravo, *Fraulein*! *Gut gemacht*! Very impressive!"

The other guests glanced nervously at one another, unsure of how to react. Moody shook his head, unable to contain his chuckle. "Sakes alive, Miss Northway. You speak German all along? How'd you keep that quiet all this time?"

"Yes, and why did you?" Kate said. "Why didn't you tell anyone? It was silly to keep this from us when my mother struggles with English, and we could have used another translator here. Papa grows weary of having to mediate whenever travelers stay," She waved her father's incoming comment away. "I know, Papa. I know. I don't need to hear your talk of preserving our heritage, all about the old country, not when we're living quite splendidly in the new one. You know, it really doesn't matter. We all know now, so there are no secrets anymore. We can converse in either language, which will suit everyone."

"But what did she say?" Monty pressed.

"Who cares about any of it?" Patience snapped. "We're all speakin' English while we're here anyway 'cause that's what most of us speak, an' I don't wanna have to have someone re-explainin' everythin' I done said an' did. Besides, your mama seems to understand everythin' so far. What's the problem?"

"Patience, for someone with your namesake, girl, you need to display some," said Finch, shooting his wife a look from across the table.

"I make no apologies for what I said, husband, and I so rightly mean it. We all speak the same language, an' Mrs. Adler here knows what we're jabberin' on about. We could be enjoyin' the rest of our supper in relative quiet-like, but we're not."

"But what on earth did you say, Miss Northway?" said Monty, his full attention on Clyde. "Please, I'm interested to hear."

The group looked at Clyde, whose sole focus was on Mr. Adler from her side of the table. She'd not wavered much since she'd spoken those words, the words that had the Adlers startled enough to realize she had undoubtedly understood everything they had said to one another. *Everything*.

And that's exactly how Clyde had hoped it would unravel, for Mr. Adler calmly said, "*Ich existiere, um den Westen zu zahmen*. I exist to tame the West. That is what she said." He leaned in, his eyes hard and cold.

"And what does this mean, Miss Northway?" He chortled, a rumbling roll of sound, deep from his belly. "You are here to educate the savages with book learning and manners? How do you intend for this to occur? Who has you do such a thing?"

Clyde, who'd since sat up straight in her chair, her back stiff, both hands now at her sides, gripping her seat, said, "You will have to ask the governess and the ward she journeyed here with, sir."

The other travelers looked in the patriarch's direction, wide-eyed with curiosity, all of them silent as if to signal an answer from him. Mr. Adler's mouth had twisted into a cruel smile verging on an outright leer.

"Or did you murder them before they could reveal such secrets to you? Where did you hide their corpses?"

Patience gasped and then quickly clamped a hand over her mouth.

Monty cleared his throat loudly, signaling his discomfort before he said, "Miss Northway, that's presumptuous . . . and *utterly* obscene. Defamatory. Hardly befitting a lady—"

But Clyde wasn't to be deterred, her focus never wavering from Mr. Adler's scowling mug. "I've not finished, Dr. Pickering. The picture on the wall in the corridor upstairs . . . It contains not one member of the Adler family sitting here, and why is that? You know, I'd even go so far as to wager 'Adler' isn't *your* family name. Please indulge me, *Herr Adler*. Am I correct in my assertion?"

Mr. Adler slammed a ham hock of a fist down sharply on the table, causing the dishes and cutlery to rattle and the guests to jerk back in their chairs. "You will not speak to me in that manner, *Fraulein*. We have opened our home to you as we have so many travelers, yet you dare disparage our hospitality, our kindness . . . our *höflichkeit*? We have given you a hot meal, a bed . . . "

"You've not answered my question, Mr. Adler. Am I correct in my assertion?"

"Miss Northway," Moody whispered. "Please stop this now. You're about to get us sent back out there."

"It would be wise to heed Mr. Evers' warning, madam," the good doctor added, shaking his head at her. "Not as if we've room and board anywhere else for the night."

"For the last time, I ask you, *am I correct in my assertion?*"

Kate sprang up from her chair, sending it sliding back, her hands braced on the table, rattling its contents. "Now, Kurt! *JETZT!*" she shouted.

There was a thunderous sound, someone striding across the floor with a purposeful, heavy gait, coming up from the dark foyer behind the good doctor's end of the table. A huge figure emerged suddenly from the pitch, a thick arm swinging a heavy implement downward, striking its target, causing a sharp, cracking sound that echoed throughout the adjoining chambers.

SIX

CLYDE PUSHED HER chair away and was up on her feet, her eyes wide in horror as she gaped at the hulking monster looming behind the good doctor's chair, working at the tool that it had brandished, attempting to get it free.

A stark silence enveloped the room as everyone stared at the once-handsome gentleman seated at the end of the table. Monty blinked a few times, as if fascinated by what he'd felt, and he gently touched the top of his head, feeling for the strange weight that was bearing down, the pressure there threatening to burst. The sledgehammer's head had caved in the top of the good doctor's skull, and the brute force of the blow had caused the face of the hammer to be embedded there, as if man and metal had simply become one. The entirety of the top of Monty's head was saturated in gore, his wavy hair a sticky, matted nest. Blood streamed down his face, painting it in rust-colored streaks. His mouth moved, attempting to form words, as he stared in Clyde's direction.

Their eyes met once again—a parting glance—as the good doctor's life slowly slipped away, his gaze growing unfocused. Clyde jumped back, her hand flailing out behind her, reaching for and then bracing against the chair she had vacated, as the giant wrenched the hammer free, splattering blood on everything and everyone, from the dishes on the table, to the clothing and faces of those seated nearest the doctor. Monty's body slumped sideways, sagging at first, before collapsing in a tired heap on the floor.

Before any of the travelers could further react to the horror that had taken the doctor's life, Mr. Adler got up from his chair, thundered towards Finch, who was still sitting there, gobsmacked, in his seat, and whipped his arm around, swiftly whisking a tiny blade, one that apparently had been hidden from plain sight, across the poor young man's neck, slicing it wide open, the skin and meat of it yawning.

Blood spurted wildly from the gaping, raw wound. Finch pawed at his throat, his voice coming out in wet, burbling gasps, causing bloody bubbles of spit to form from his lips.

Patience started shrieking when she realized where the hot spatter that landed on her skin and dress had come from. Finch tugged weakly at her shoulder, trying to get her to lean in towards him as he babbled at her. His attempts to get her to help him were short-lived, however, as his head clattered down face-first, onto his dish, still half-full of potatoes and dumplings now mingling with blood and the brown murk of the last traces of stew.

There was a grinding sound of metal on metal, gears clanking, from somewhere below the table. Clyde caught sight of Mrs. Adler who, during the bloody commotion, had snuck off to a darkened corner of the dining room. There she quietly stood, watching the events unfold, having just pulled at a wooden lever on the wall.

The floor let out a rumbling groan as it opened its mouth wide underneath the good doctor's chair and swallowed him and his chair whole. Before Clyde could reach him, Mr. Adler whisked around the table and joined the giant in pulling Finch's body, prying it from Patience's grasp. They dragged Finch's prone form to the hole and roughly rolled him over and shoved him down it. Patience, still screaming for her husband, was up and out of her seat, about to lunge for the Adler men.

Moody, on the other hand, had been in stealthy defense mode since the attack, as he grabbed Patience from around the waist, pinning her arms to her sides and lifting her, spinning them both around. He set her down and then pulled them in the direction of the kitchen. Mrs. Adler stepped in front of them, blocking them from the kitchen and aiming a derringer at the center of Moody's face. She shook her head and clicked her tongue at Moody, who pulled Patience back and directly behind him, her human shield.

The others were not going to reach Clyde without a fight. She would see to it. She pulled out a hairpin, sharp and gleaming, from her updo, and was already moving quickly around the table, her arm reaching out, hand grappling for the back of Kate's collar. She yanked Kate backwards towards her and then locked her in a chokehold. Holding the hairpin's pointy end at Kate's jugular, Clyde spun around with Kate to face the Adler men who looked as if they were about to make a move towards Patience and Moody.

Mrs. Adler let out an audible gasp at the sight of

Kate who'd been so swiftly turned hostage. She aimed the derringer at Clyde, shouting a command at her husband. Mr. Adler took two steps towards Clyde and Kate, but Clyde turned and faced him, making a show of digging the tip of the hairpin just hard enough to draw a trickle of blood from Kate's neck, causing Kate to titter.

The charming Adler lady was their way out for the time being.

Moody and Patience joined Clyde and her struggling, laughing hostage, warily watching between the Adler men and Mrs. Adler with the pistol shaking in her grip.

"*Mutti, erschieße sie,*" Kate hissed. "Shoot her in her pretty head!"

Clyde whipped around, her arm lock around Kate, constricting. She stared directly at the Adler matriarch, her eyes practically daring the woman to fire. "You do that, and you'll miss with that useless little thing in your hand. You're more likely to hit your darling Kate. You wouldn't want that, would you, *Frau* Adler? You know, that even sounds strange on the tongue. *Adler.* It doesn't match the surroundings."

"Miss Northway, best hold your tongue," Moody said from the side of his mouth. "They don't look as if they like whatever it is you're implyin'."

Clyde chortled, her gaze never faltering from Mrs. Adler. "Son, you think I give a good goddamn what these fine folks think? Bunch of liars and killers? You must know *Adler* isn't their real family name."

"As far as I'm concerned, Miss Northway, they can be Adlers, Paddlers, Rattlers . . . I don't rightly care. In the moment, what I *do* care about is gettin' outta here alive. Don't you wanna do that, Miss Northway?" Moody said, his voice edged with worry.

Mrs. Adler cocked the hammer, the drawn-out, clicking sound of it echoing throughout the room. Clyde dug the pointed end of the pin into the wound on Kate's neck. Kate let out a jittery bleat, like she'd forgotten how to laugh or cry aloud and didn't quite know which she wanted to express in the heat of the moment.

Mr. Adler stepped forward, edging closer to the tightly bunched group. He had his hands out, waving them in submission. Moody took a step back, bringing Patience with him, moving closer to Clyde and her hostage.

"If you dare harm my daughter, *Fraulein*," he said, "you and your fellow travelers will be chopped into tiny pieces and fed to *meine schweine*."

The hulking Adler son emitted a wet whuffle of a sound, a cackle from what Clyde surmised. She doubted the creature actually had it in him to laugh like a human. His grin stretched his pasty, flat face, threatening to rip its doughy exterior. The Adlers closed in on the little group.

But it was Patience's warning screech, "Look out!" followed by sharp blow to the back of Clyde's head that made Clyde drop the hairpin . . .

She collapsed on the floor, the deep scarlet heat of the darkness taking hold.

SEVEN

MUTTI PROMISED ME, PROMISED me that I could have the red dress when they finished.

If you know this dress, if you have *seen* this dress, you would want it for yourself. You would. I know you would. I would hide it away in *Mutti's* sewing room. I love that we have such a house that has a real sewing room *and* a salon. I've seen salons in picture books, never like this. This has been the largest house on our travels, with so many places to hide, places where I can see things happening from the shadows.

I prefer the empty rooms. They miss me when I leave them. When I'm there, they grow excited; they whisper secrets to me, secrets I promised I would tell no one. Some of their secrets I've known for a long time, for as long as we have lived here. Some of the secrets are kept in shadows and smell of rot and waste. Others share terrible things about *Mutti und Vati*. They don't need to share anything with me; I tell them I already know. I see and hear everything.

For instance, I know that *Mutti und Vati* have something *schrecklich* planned for the women, the loud one with the baby growing inside of her and the

one, *die Dame* with the red dress. *Das schöne Kleid.*
I get to keep her dress.

I imagine the silk will feel cool underneath my
fingers. It will smell of fresh flowers, lady sweat, and
afternoon walks with gentlemen callers. The bustle
will crinkle and bend when I gently push it. I've no
womanly shape, no curves and slopes, so I know the
dress will feel unnatural when I may finally wear it,
tight in places where it shouldn't be, but it will only
be on me.

Ich wünschte ich wäre hübsch. I long to be pretty.
Such women can have the world, if they desire. Here
in the prairie, their beauty doesn't last. The sun and
wind turn their skin rough and wrinkled, their eyes
grey like the dead sky. "Stay indoors," says *Mutti*,
"The air outside *ist grausam gegenüber Frauen.*" So
cruel to women. *Mutti* knows.

I could never be like *Mutti*. The land has turned
her *kalt und bitter*. No wonder *Vati* will not touch her
the way he once did. I remember, when I was a child,
hearing their passion in their bed. That was many
years ago when we lived in the dirt house, one that
seemed a part of the earth, our first house in the new
land. We had travelers stay often. Then one night, a
particular traveler joined us. A gentleman with curly
red hair and a thick laugh that stayed with us long
after the evening had broken. It wasn't his handsome
looks or charming demeanor that had *Mutti und Vati
verzaubert,* their eyes gleaming with excitement. It
was the heavy brown bag he carried and kept with
him during his stay, the one clinking with house
treasures and trinkets in silver and gold.

"Reichtum macht Männer verrückt," meine Oma

said when *Vati* told her we were leaving for the new country.

She was right. Treasure makes men mad. There, in that tiny dirt house with its one room divided by a single curtain, the dining table had been set for our family and guests. It was then when *Vati* had *mein Bruder* stand behind the sheet with a hammer in his hand, while the gentleman guest shared stories with *meine schwester und Mutti und Vati*. I was not permitted to watch; instead, I was told to stay behind the curtain until it was over. I didn't know what "it" meant until I heard the grunt and then the awful cracking sound of something fragile being broken.

After *meine Schwester* sang me to sleep that night, I dreamed of *mein Bruder* in our house breaking big, wooden crates open with his hammer with that same cracking noise echoing in my dream. Inside the crates were crimson jellies that jiggled and then burst with hot, copper liquid that filled the house until it couldn't breathe anymore.

That house, it just drowned.

I *still* dream this every night. But I don't let it worry me.

Instead, I remember the red dress, and all is well again.

It was the sharp, throbbing pain in her head that brought Clyde back to the land of the living. The sweet stench of tangy copper and rotting meat caused her to recoil against her bonds. The wound on the back of her head pulsed, sending a searing slice throughout her skull, spreading to the back of her neck and down her spine.

The first thing she saw in the flickering, hazy orange gloom was a face. A face that took up the entirety of her line of vision. She remembered the face. It wasn't particularly attractive. Its muddy green eyes were dull, the white of the left reddened with ruddy capillaries. The skin was smooth and pale with freckles along the bridge of the pert, little nose, until the skin reached the apex of the corner of the mouth. That scarring turned the skin shiny and unnaturally taut. One side of the lips had been fused over with scarred skin as if it had been soldered together. The other half of the lips were chapped with red-crusted flakes that had been loosened enough that if Clyde were to rub a thumb across them, they'd come right off, leaving the skin underneath pink and raw, exposed to the elements.

The face belonged to the youngest of the clan, the mute who'd thought she could hide in the shadows of the house. Clyde had seen the skittish creature dart out of the room next to the bedroom she'd shared with the young bride and mother-to-be, Patience.

Patience.

The driver. Moody.

Where were they? And why hadn't the shotgun—what was his name? Something odd on the tongue that suited his standoffish demeanor. Where was he? Leartus? Yes, that was it. Leartus Shurchell.

"Dead, right? He's dead," she said aloud, startling herself with the strange sound of it. Her voice had been chalky-thick when she spoke, and her mouth felt as if it had been stuffed and dried with wads of cotton.

They'd had her gagged with something earlier, something that tasted of dirt and leather.

The skittish thing who'd been in a crouch in front of her, peering at her face, gave her a little half-smile. It was really all she could manage, Clyde supposed. Clyde tried getting up from whatever it was that had her down, but it held her tightly, constricting her arms back.

She'd been tied to a chair. Her twisting only served to make the itchy rope tighter around her wrists. A rope burn had already formed around her wrist, the one unbound from a brace, smarting with the heat of it. Clyde whipped her head around as far as she could turn it, causing the tendons to pop loudly in her ears. All she wanted was to get a good look at her surroundings. The light in the area was weak, emanating from both a lantern and low flames puttering in a fireplace, casting little more than a feeble orange glow.

The scarred girl pulled herself up from her crouch to stretch, the only sound coming from her a tiny purr that rumbled through her slight figure. She spun around and practically skipped over to the long wooden table against the wall in front of Clyde. There were tools hanging from nails in the wall, all of them old and rusty from lack of adequate care. The scarred girl lightly trailed her hand over each instrument, as if carefully considering which one to select. She went back and forth between one and another before she turned back to Clyde who was watching her intently.

Both Clyde and the scarred girl were suddenly wrenched from their staring standoff when a grating shriek pierced the silence.

"Finch Henry! FINCH!" howled Patience from somewhere in the darkest area of the room, a place where the gloomy light of the lantern on the table couldn't reach.

Clyde could only just make out the young bride's silhouette. Patience's body twisted and turned, her barely perceptible shadow on the wall behind her writhing there in a mad half-dance. She had been bound to a chair as well and didn't seem as if she was going to take it much more without a snakelike fight between her and her binding.

"Mrs. Wilkson, stop struggling," Clyde hissed. "You'll only make it worse."

"Where did they take my husband?" the girl sobbed. "Where is he?"

"They killed him. Don't you remember?"

Patience's body went rigid at Clyde's words, her voice catching then slowly forming into a pitiful wail that escalated in pitch, causing Clyde to wince.

"Mrs. Wilkson, you have to stop."

"I want to see my husband. I want to see him!"

"Calm yourself. You'll anger our captors. Do you want to provoke them after what they did to your husband and Dr. Pickering? Do you remember what they did to the doctor?"

"I don't care. They can do away with me too. I want to be with him. I want to be with my husband!"

"Mrs. Wilkson, please. You're with child. Do you wish for your baby to be harmed as well?"

Patience's wailing formed into a warbling stream of soft sobs causing the outline of her body to slightly judder there in the dark.

Once she calmed herself, she whispered, "Why . . .
Why are we here? What are they gonna do to us?"

Clyde turned back to the scarred girl who still had
on that sad, faraway half-smile. The girl shook her
head in disapproval at Clyde, as if trying to share a
moment of empathetic support. Clyde merely
returned the girl's smile with a wolfish one of her own,
lips curling, baring her teeth at the girl.

Meanwhile, behind her chair, Clyde was working
diligently at the rope that bound her wrists. Using the
side of her opposite hand, she could just skim the
wrist line of her arm with the strange brace, rubbing
it against a particularly hard knot of material there.
She kept her eyes on the scarred girl who had since
made her way over to the dying fire and picked up a
fireplace poker. The girl prodded at the burnt logs
that had since gone charred and smoky. A tiny flame
crackled from the kindling underneath and was
released, catching the logs, broadening in scope and
washing the entire room in flickering light.

At first, Clyde was startled by the actual size of the
room, if one thought "room" was the appropriate term
for it. They were definitely underground, undoubtedly
under the house. Probably even just under the dining
room floor where the trap door had been. She couldn't
see signs of it on the ceiling, but upon further
inspection of the place, she could make out a doorway
with no door leading to a black space, a mouth of
nothingness that beckoned.

The room was a man-made cavernous space with
arched ceilings, its foundation constructed with stone.
At first, Clyde wasn't certain about its purpose as it
seemed lacking in care. However, the space itself was

large enough to craft an entire living quarters should a family have need for it. As it was, it was nothing more than a yawning cave with a few chairs, a tool table, and the fireplace, which was the strangest aspect of the place, the only element of the room that had been especially created, one that had Clyde surmise that the cave *was* a manmade "room." The smoke from the fire the scarred girl had revived hadn't sullied the air, so, obviously, there was a flue opened where most of the smoke could escape.

The actual *purpose* of the room was unclear until Clyde discovered the source of the bitingly sweet stench of decay that underscored the smoke. And it was in that exact moment that Patience had seen it too. Her grating scream ripped the room apart, echoing throughout, causing Clyde's ears to ring in protest.

The other occupants of the room, also bound to several chairs, were moldering corpses, some of which were barely recognizable as human, still clad in their travel wear. The one nearest Clyde had once been a gentleman as it had on a bloodstained and dust-coated proper suit complete with waistcoat and bowtie. Its body had festered there. The head bore a giant hole at the side of its skull that was crawling with maggots. Its one open eye had since dried in its socket, its permanent wink a morbid remnant of its once-human state. A much smaller corpse, clad in a Sunday dress had been placed beside the one next to Clyde and had deliberately been set there, for Clyde could see the evident relationship between the two, almost as if a sickening reminder to its murdering captors. Unlike its adult counterpart, the smaller corpse was headless, and its little hands had been gripping the arms of the chair it was bound to.

The little one's dress.

Clyde twisted around to get a better look at it. She had seen it before. The delicate pinafore over the gingham.

Before she could react, Clyde was shaken by the pitch in Patience's voice, the young woman's screams having formed into wracking sobs. Clyde shot a biting glare in Patience's direction. She silently cursed herself for failing to see they'd been granted more company. Mrs. Adler must have come from somewhere beyond the darkened doorway. The woman had taken the poker from the scarred girl, who had since sat on the tool table, legs dangling and swinging over the edge, hands set to either side of her with palms flat on the table. She still had that sad half-smile, her gaze far away.

"Please don't do . . . .Please . . . I'm sorry. I just want to see my husband. You understand? I want to be with him," whimpered Patience. "You speak English real good, so I know you understand me. *Please* let me be with him. I don't care what you do to me as long as I can be with him."

Mrs. Adler merely grunted in response as she focused on heating the poker in the flames.

Clyde then knew exactly what was coming and suddenly felt powerless in the moment, even though she had fared far worse predicaments. She had known women like this, the ones who meted out painful punishment that was lasting and unforgiving. The scarred girl clapped her hands with glee as Mrs. Adler brought the poker over in Patience's direction, her mouth twisted in a tight, cruel smile. Just as Patience's whimpering formed into another wail, Mrs. Adler squeezed the young woman's lips shut between her free hand's pinching fingers and brought the searing poker tip to one corner of Patience's mouth. The flesh beneath the poker sizzled. Mrs. Adler scowled as Patience frantically twisted against her bonds, whimpering, tears rolling down her cheeks in rivulets.

"You must be silent, *Mädchen* . . . like a mouse in our house," Mrs. Adler said. She drew the poker away and let go of Patience's mouth.

Patience slumped back in the chair, wheezing through one side of her mouth, just before she gave into the black, her body going limp. Her once-pretty face was a wet mess of snot and tears. Sweat had beaded on her brow causing her hair to cling to her forehead in sticky, stringy strands. And her lips . . .

The poker had welded one corner of her mouth shut, the skin having bubbled over and melded together. There was a raw pink strip running from just beneath one nostril to her chin from where the poker had settled.

Clyde felt Patience's anguish from where she sat. That white, hot pain that shot through the nervous system and inevitably forced the body to give up and give in. She knew that sort of agony far too well. She also knew the sort of stock from which Mrs. Adler, or whoever she actually was, hailed. Women like Mrs. Adler were born into that cruelty, so they knew nothing else.

Some even learned to *enjoy* it.

So, naturally, Clyde figured it wouldn't be so bad

if she taught the woman a painful lesson of her own. It was what women like Mrs. Adler understood, after all, the universal language of suffering. There was nothing quite like it.

Clyde understood that too.

Sometimes, dare she admit, she also took pleasure in it.

When Mrs. Adler turned in her direction and made her way over, poker still in hand, Clyde twisted her wrist at just the right spot for her other hand to rub in the right place. She slid the knotty material back, pulling the leather strip casing the metal that made up her arm brace.

Mrs. Adler sighed down at Clyde, turning the poker this way and that in her grip. "Now then, *Fraulein,* and what are we to do with *you*?"

"Good question," said Clyde. "*Mal sehen was passiert*, shall we?"

Clyde's fingers that had been looped to the brace yanked sharply. There was an odd, metallic click from behind Clyde's chair, like something had activated and snapped open. She grimaced, her shoulders rolling, as she roughly twisted her arms in their bonds. She jerked the shoulder bearing the braced arm, and as she did, there was the soft, slow hiss of something tearing, and Clyde gasped, wheezing sharply at the exertion.

Curiosity having gotten the better of her, Mrs. Adler stepped around Clyde, bending over to see what it was she had been working on behind her chair. "*Was ist das*?" She craned her neck to get a closer look.

With a swift jerk, Clyde wrenched her arm free

and drove it upwards, the blades that had been previously hidden in her brace embedding right into the bottom of Mrs. Adler's chin, getting caught there. Mrs. Adler's eyes went round in shock. Blood filled her mouth, and she gurgled and coughed. One of the larger blades had pierced through her mouth and skewered up through her tongue, forcing her to keep her mouth wide open.

Clyde yanked her arm down, bringing Mrs Adler with it, causing the matronly woman to wobble against Clyde. Mrs. Adler's hands grabbed at Clyde's neckline in a weak attempt to gain a chokehold on her, but Clyde shrugged off Mrs. Adler's flailing hands, twisting about. She shook the ropes free from her other hand, and with a swift, downwards yank of her arm, she freed the bladed brace from Mrs. Adler's shredded chin, causing Mrs. Adler to pitch forward, the bulky weight of her body sagging against Clyde. The woman's blood splattered all over Clyde's face and sleeve.

Grimacing, Clyde roughly shoved Mrs. Adler away from her, sending the woman sprawling backwards onto the dirt floor. Clyde then reached down to untie the ropes binding each of her ankles to the chair's front legs. As Mrs. Adler drew herself up from the floor, cupping a bloody hand over the shredded lower portion of her face, Clyde was nearly free, hurriedly working at the right ankle's bindings.

Mrs. Adler staggered once again towards Clyde who was pulling the last of the ropes away. "Ooo arrrrr a guesss in arrr houu . . . " She said around a fresh bout of blood that was rapidly filling her mouth. She spat out the blood directly at Clyde's feet, sprinkling the tops of her boots.

Clyde turned to look up only to find the big woman looming over her.

Mrs. Adler's blood-stained hands curled into knotty fists at her side. She let the excess blood run from her mouth, down her sliced chin and aproned front. When she leered, wide-mouthed, at Clyde, the blood flow kept coming, pouring from her open mouth. She gurgled, clearing it from her mouth again, and then spat it directly in Clyde's face, causing Clyde to draw back, her face bunched in disgust.

"You arrrr a guesss in our house, lil' mouse." She drew back a fist and swung at Clyde's face.

Clyde deftly caught the fist, trapping it in her hand, squeezing it, and she pulled up out of her chair, kicking the last of the rope away as she did. "Yes, but this isn't *your* house, now is it?"

She sunk the blades of the brace into Mrs. Adler's throat, tugging at it and ripping it wide open. Blood sprayed, splattering over Clyde, the chair, the floor, and the wall. Clyde shoved the woman away. Mrs. Adler clawed at her neck, her voice coming in rasping burbles. She let out a wet snort before she crumbled in a matted, gory heap on the floor.

With a swipe of her other hand, Clyde flattened back the blades of her brace, locking them in once more, almost as if they'd never appeared. She patted down her dress and then wiped back the sticky strands of hair from her face, as if it made a difference. That overt sense of pride, however, had been engrained in her since she was a child. Even when situations called for violent means, she still had it in her to be dignified. She looked around the room, turning on her heel as she did. The scarred girl had silently left the room, having scurried away while Clyde and Mrs. Adler had been . . . *distracted*.

The stillness that permeated the wide room after Mrs. Adler had been dealt with broke with the soft, mewling sounds coming from Patience. Clyde moved quickly towards her and then worked at untying the girl from her chair.

"Whatever happens here," Clyde softly said as she removed the ropes from Patience's feet, "follow me closely, and don't stray. Understand?"

Patience nodded, wide-eyed. A bubble of snot formed in one nostril, and she sniffed it back, causing her to cough. She tried to speak, but it was evident the pain around her lips was too much as she winced at the attempt.

Patience's facial expression signaled enough of a hint, and Clyde was ashamed she was somewhat grateful for the horror the girl had endured since it would keep her from screaming. This would keep things simple and silent.

Clyde patted Patience on the knee and then went to work on the bindings around the girl's wrists, frantically pulling at them. "I don't know where we are, but I don't think it would be foolish to presume we're under the house . . . dining room, kitchen, somewhere around there. I suggest we see where that tunnel leads." She pulled away the remaining ropes from Patience's right wrist and gently urged the girl up on her feet.

Clyde then picked up the poker that Mrs. Adler had dropped as the lower portion of her face had been ripped to ribbons. When she turned back to Patience, who was standing there directly behind her, uncertain of what to do, Patience recoiled at the sight of the poker.

Clyde immediately realized her mistake in taking it, so she held it out to Patience. "You will overcome that fear when you wield what hurt you." She took Patience by the hand and pulled Patience in towards her and placed the poker in her hands, wrapping the girl's fingers around it. "Do *not* show them any weakness. That only serves to bolster them."

Patience looked down at the poker, now a weapon, in her grip. Her knuckles whitened around it. Clyde gently wrapped her hands over the girl's, breaking Patience's daze. Her wild-eyed stare locked with Clyde's eyes. Clyde guided the girl's hands, placing them as if wielding the weapon.

"The hand here is your spearing hand. You thrust with it," Clyde said, squeezing Patience's hand at the midpoint of the poker. "The one here at the top, you keep it a little loose. That's your guide, your control."

"Wike a wifle," whispered Patience, nodding, wincing around her wound.

"Much like a rifle, yes, but without firing it, of course. That would change its purpose entirely. Although, a fireplace poker masquerading as a firearm could be . . . strangely useful at the very least." Clyde offered the girl a grin. "Even a little fun."

It worked, calming her. Patience softly chuckled.

Clyde let go of Patience's hands and watched the girl practice spearing the air with the poker. She then walked over to the table against the wall, looking over the tools there and the ones dangling from hooks. She picked up a butcher knife and a skinning knife from the table, turning them around, examining their sharpness against her finger. Then something else caught her eye, something directly in her line of sight.

Actually, it was a pair of somethings, both having been placed deliberately aligned, dangling there, nails keeping them braced against the wall.

Two hatchets. One having been evidently sharped and cleaned, its blade edge gleaming in the firelight. Its partner had seen some action, its own edge crusted over with old blood.

"Ahhh . . . 'iss Northway?" Patience managed to say.

Clyde froze, her head turning ever so slightly in Patience's direction.

"Who *are* you?"

Clyde ignored the question, turning back to the twin beauties in front of her, teasing her there. She carefully took the clean hatchet from the wall and then swung it around, testing its weight, her arm loosely pinwheeling. Patience stood there, eyes round at the sight of the woman practicing with her new weaponry.

"The monsters in this house need to be put in their place, my dear Mrs. Wilkson," said Clyde as she swung her arm around, slicing the air with the hatchet. "And, unfortunately, we are the ones burdened with that responsibility." She spun around, facing Patience, who jumped back, startled, gripping the poker tightly to her.

"Keep that fear an active participant tonight. It will keep you alive," Clyde said. "Ready?"

Patience swallowed, nodded.

"Good. Now follow me, and whatever you do, don't stray."

EIGHT

THERE IS NO time to mourn for deine Mutti, meine Kinder. We still have much to do.

Vati says this when we tell him what has happened, yet we have always mourned the dead. Now we are expected to keep going as if *Mutti* had not suffered at the hands of *die Dame im roten Kleid*.

That red dress. It's mine, after I've taken her life.

For now, we'll wait for her and the *idiotisches Mädchen*, the one ripe with child, to reveal themselves. The idiot girl will be easy. It's the lady in the red dress who is lethal and prepared.

Now I ask you, what kind of a woman, what such lady, is prepared to fight?

Schnell und gerissen, my child, says *Vati. She is quick and cunning, like a lioness circling her prey. So we must assume she is observing everything. She is learning the terrain.*

She doesn't know everything, *Vati*. She won't be prepared for me.

Vati laughs, not at me, not in jest. He isn't cruel like *Mutti*. *Vati* laughs as if he and I are the only people left in the world, and the strange things that happen in that world are the secret we share. He knows I mean what I say, and he likes that about me.

My brave one. Oh, my dearest brave one, he says, smiling, *Du wirst dein rotes Kleid haben.*
You will have your red dress.

Clyde had quickly, and somewhat haphazardly, crafted a makeshift belt out of rope and the remnants of her dress overlay that she used to sheath and strap down the hatchet to her side. She'd need it at waist level, within easy reach

After all, a lady always came prepared for a solitary war, even if that meant temporarily losing her dignity in the process.

She hadn't done the same with Patience's weapon, however, so she had Patience bind the poker to her own back. "Should you need it, you'll be behind me, so it will be of ready convenience there in front of you," she said as Patience tested the poker's bonds. The poker slid up and down in her grasp. "Hold from its center, and gently guide it upwards and out rather than downwards," Clyde instructed. "That way it won't catch on any material. Test it now. See if you're able to remove it quickly before you wield it."

Patience did as she was told, practicing, and by the fourth attempt, she was able to remove the weapon swiftly from its cradle against Clyde's back.

Clyde turned, nodding, eyes once again locking on her companion's wide, pallid face. "That'll do. Understand there will be no time to think. In predicaments like this, let instinct be your guide, as awful as it is to stomach."

She led Patience into the dark. They crept swiftly

and silently down the tunnel until they found the ladder quite possibly leading up to an interior portion of the house. It hadn't been as easy to find as they'd initially thought. The tunnel out of the torture room twisted this way and that, narrowing down further and darkening as they went.

Clyde put a hand out, bracing flat against Patience's breastbone, halting the girl. The girl was out of breath, gasping in the dark behind her.

"Breathe in and then let it out slowly," said Clyde, who gave the girl a quick shoulder squeeze. "It will ease your pulse and calm you. You'll feel much better."

Patience nodded, taking in a deep breath and then slowly exhaling. She felt as if her heart had been lit on fire, and her body turned to jelly. Her knees wobbled as she leaned heavily against the tunnel wall. The only light in that tunnel sifted through the cracks in the trapdoor above them at the top of the ladder attached to the wall. The ladder was rickety, some of its wooden steps having grown black with rot.

Directly above them, rumbling shouts could be heard. The sudden sound of it caused Patience to gasp and clamp her hands over her mouth. She seemed about to say something, stepping forward as she did, but with her eyes steady on the trapdoor, Clyde held out a warning finger at the girl.

There was a shrill yelp of someone crying out in pain, followed by a heavy thump on the trapdoor, as if something bulky had dropped upon it.

"Had to have been Evers," muttered Clyde. She turned to Patience, her eyes hard. "No matter what happens, focus solely on me, girl. Hear? Move where I do and stay close."

Hyperventilating, Patience looked as if she was about to faint, her face wan.

Clyde took the girl's sweaty hand in her own, giving it a light squeeze. "When we're able to go, follow my path up exactly as I've done, one rung at a time. Nod if you understand."

Patience nodded, but her gaping stare kept darting back and forth, from the trapdoor to Clyde then back again. There was a howl directly above them, and something was then dragged across the trapdoor, the soft hiss of movement causing the two women to exhale, the air escaping their lungs in a sigh. Clyde let go of Patience's hand and put her palm out in front of the younger woman, signaling her not to move, not just yet. A conversation was carrying on above them, the low, rumbling voice of a man and the soft patter, the tinkle of laughter from a woman, one practiced in evening flirtation and charm.

Clyde's eyes narrowed at the sound of it. She kept her hand out, bracing Patience, her finger held up once again. She put that finger to her lips and then pointed upwards, signaling the younger woman that she was still waiting on the ones above. The two of them listened, their breathing hushed. They waited until the conversation above had stopped and there was nothing but the constant drum of their heartbeat in their ears.

Urging Patience to follow her lead, Clyde quickly began removing layers of her dress from its ripped overskirt all the way down to the chemise and the petticoat covering the skeleton of the bustle. She then rid herself of the crinolette that had since lost its shape, its cage-like shape having bent. Once she was free from the excess layers of her dress, she pulled on the flattened underskirt and buttoned on the bodice jacket. She turned back to the ladder and quickly moved, one leg stepping up, her body hefting up the ladder, the rung creaking under her weight.

Clyde sensed something was wrong as there was no movement behind her, so she twisted her head, peering over her shoulder and wincing at the effort. Patience was still rooted to her spot, seeming unable to move, gaping up at the older woman who dangled there, holding tightly to the railings.

"You need to stop your dawdling and move, girl," Clyde said, motioning with her head.

It was as if Patience had woken up from a dream and had realized reality was none too kind. Her expression sagged, her eyes brimming with tears. She struggled around her burned lips. "He's dead," she whispered. "They killed 'im. Done cut his froat, didn't they? He didn't do *nothin*', and they killed 'im . . . What they kill 'im fo', 'iss Northway? D'you know? An' the doctor? Kindly a gent as any. This ain't right. *They* ain't right."

All Clyde could manage in the moment was a slight nod in Patience's direction, her mouth tight-lined.

"They ain't right," Patience repeated, her face crinkling in disgust.

That part, the reminder of the madness, was what stabbed Clyde in her stomach.

"Are we gonna kill 'em?" Patience asked.

Clyde was quiet for what seemed a long moment, the dark breaking between them before she answered

"Yes, for your husband, for the good doctor, and for all the rest, we're going to kill them."

That was all Patience needed to hear.

NINE

THE TRAPDOOR, which appeared to open on the kitchen, was trickier to open than Clyde initially assumed. It wasn't due to a weight upon it. A body had certainly fallen on it earlier, but the door itself wasn't difficult to open. It was caught due to the latch keeping it shut, an elaborate twist of iron looped in a hook and chain attached to the floorboard. Clyde could only get the door open a couple of inches before it caught, sticking there. The low, yellow lantern light in the kitchen flickered, casting strange shadows that danced and disappeared, danced and disappeared, teasing its presence, flirting with anyone wishing to have a look.

Clyde could just make out the legs of the stove from where she peered out from beneath the floor. She tried pushing hard at the door, using the top of her head and free hand to attempt to wrench it free from its bonds.

Luckily, she didn't have to.

The trapdoor was suddenly unlatched and slammed open with enough force that it rattled her teeth. It was just before a man's huge, hairy hand reached down and painfully snatched her by her loose bun, yanking her up and out of the hole.

Clyde cried out, her hands clawing at the grip of the man pulling her up into the kitchen. Dangling by her hair, she felt ripping at the roots.

"What do we have here? Such a difficult woman. You are much like my wife, so stubborn, *so lästig*," said Mr. Adler as he spun her around, wrenching her arm behind her back as he did, pirouetting them in the direction of the stove. "You remember my wife, don't you, *Fraulein*? And you left her down there to bleed *wie ein feststeckendes Schwein* . . . like a stuck pig. This is true then, yes? Did you cut her throat? Did you enjoy her pain? Did you like watching her die?"

Clyde squirmed in his grasp, flailing about, her jaw clenching and unclenching, cringing at the pinching pain when he yanked her head back, his fingers still wrapped in her hair. She let out a wheezing snicker that then formed into a loud string of laughter bubbling out from deep within her chest.

"You're laughing?" Mr. Adler pulled the poker from its binding against her back and tossed it away, and Clyde heard the loud clink of it when it hit the floor. Then Mr. Adler wrenched her forward and shoved her head down, holding it mere inches away from the stovetop, one hand gripping the back of her neck as he held her arm behind her back with his other.

The heat from the stove was suffocating. She brought her free arm, the bound one with the bladed brace, to her side, her hand grasping for the handle of the hatchet in its sheath. Her movements caused her arm ever so briefly to skim the scorching surface of the stove, a bit of skin exposed on the side of her wrist burning. She quickly drew her arm away to her side,

Then Kate drove the tip back in, this time, wiggling it around violently, as if she was broadening the wound she'd created in Patience's abdomen. "That's a good girl," she whispered as she moved the tip around and around in Patience's middle, her voice honey and smoke as she spoke. "It's a sin to have a baby grow up in the middle of all this hell. You want what's best for it, don't you?"

Clyde promptly sheathed the bloody hatchet to her side once more and got on her feet. In a couple of quick strides, she was at Kate's back, one hand out, reaching for its intended target, the parasol's handle. Before Kate could slide the tip out of Patience's abdomen, Clyde had yanked at the parasol's handle from underneath Kate's elbow, revealing the slim sword blade the handle had sheathed.

Startled by the movement behind her, Kate pulled frantically at the tip of the parasol, only to discover it was stuck there . . .

. . . as Clyde sandwiched Kate between her and Patience, driving the sword blade into Kate's back and through her body. The tip of the blade poked through Kate's upper abdomen, and as the light left Patience's eyes, Patience managed one barely perceptible chortle just before she went limp, her body sagging against Kate's.

Clyde hooked an arm around Kate's neck, pulling the young woman in towards her. "That's *mine*, dear," Clyde said in Kate's ear and then slid the blade from her.

Kate let out a startled gasp, just as the weight of Patience's limp body became too much for her to bear. Clyde stepped back, letting the two women—one dead, one slowly dying—collapse on the floor in a tangled heap.

Clyde slipped the blade back into the parasol's handle, and then set the parasol against the wall. Dipping into a low crouch, she took a long look at the two women, one of them breathing in tight gasps, puffs of breath. She then gently nudged Patience's prone form, rolling it off Kate, whose eyes had grown watery. Her hands cupped the raw wound in her middle, the front of her dress bloomed with red. Clyde brushed back the young woman's hair from her face. She gently took Kate's hand in her own, letting the tar-like blood seep from Kate's middle. Kate weakly attempted to pry her hand away from Clyde's grip, but Clyde shook her head at her, shushing her and stroking the young woman's hand with her thumb.

"*Hör auf damit, kleines Mädchen.* You stop that right now. You're losing blood. It's how it needs to be," she said to the dying woman.

Kate attempted to speak, but the words refused to form. Instead, it came out as a cough, strong enough to spatter sprinkles of blood and bile over Clyde's face and neck. The young woman tried again to pull her hand free, but this time, Clyde brought it to her body, holding it tightly against her. She held her other hand down firmly against Kate's chest, preventing Kate from moving further.

"Your family doesn't belong here," Clyde said. Her words belied her tone, which had gone soft and soothing. "This is what you all do, isn't it? Isolate travelers here, or wherever it is you settle, just before you commit to slaughtering innocents. Just before the butchery. What, do you do this to collect whatever bounty you find? I'd wager you'd have quite the time with a Wells Fargo stage if you all had been remotely cunning in your pursuits . . . and yet . . . I don't think it's about the thievery. Not at all."

Her hand lingering there over Kate's heart, Clyde could feel the young woman's pulse slowing down, little by little, until it was barely perceptible.

Kate's eyes held Clyde's steady gaze. There was a flicker of something there. A spark of amusement, the fine skin crinkling at the corners. The young woman's mouth had gone slack, a fine string of red drool dangling from one corner.

"You and your family . . . You *enjoyed* it, didn't you?"

But by then, Kate's eyes had glazed over, staring into the void.

"You did. You enjoyed inflicting pain," Clyde said, her tone having formed sharp edges. "Savagery. Nothing but savagery." With a grimace, Clyde let go of Kate's hand, letting the young woman's arm hit the floor.

Clyde staggered up on her feet, but before she could turn around, the screeching wail coming up from behind her came with a blunt force and knocked her sideways, sending her slamming back down to the floor.

TEN

I AM NOT supposed to cry. Tears are not for adults, *Vati* told me. Tears are *für Kinder*. Adults do not cry when they suffer. They suffer quietly.

Wir halten unseren Schmerz. We hold our pain.

I do not hold my pain. Instead, I have put my pain deep in a cave where no one else can find it, a cave inside of me. Only a demon will find that pain; only a demon will dig it out of its cave and eat it.

The lady with her red dress. *Sie isst Schmerz.* She eats pain.

She is like the witch in the faerie stories Kate would tell us during the dark winters when the snow turned everything silent, and the moon made us ghosts. The witch would frighten men with her beauty and then kill them with her poisoned words.

Sometimes, the witch would eat women and their children, too.

This is also the reason why the lady in the red dress is so dangerous. She would eat children if she could. Crunch their bones between her neat, white teeth. Suck out the marrow with her rosy lips. Feast on their little hearts. Adorn her neck with their tiny hands and feet.

Maybe the source of her power is in her dress.
I think it may be.
Rid her of the dress, and she will be easy to kill.
Das Kleid gehört mir. Her dress, all mine.

Clyde was being dragged by one leg along the muddy path leading to the barn, her dress riding up her backside, pulling at the doughy wet earth, sliding it along with her.

It took her a good minute to rationalize her predicament, the second blackout of the evening. Her back was on fire, sending waves of pain up her spine to her neck. Something had struck her there. She cursed herself under her breath. She had foolishly neglected, once more, to adhere to one particular lesson that had been drilled into her for years from when she was a girl learning the ways of cruelty and discipline, being molded into the woman she was.

That lesson, so seemingly simple, was the most difficult for her and obviously continued to be.

That lesson: One must always assume the enemy is *everywhere*. Because of this, *she must be alert from all sides*.

And that included the rear.

When she craned her head up to see whomever was holding onto her, all she could discern was a mountainous shadow, a fortress of a humanoid shape. Clyde twisted her body this way and that in an attempt to loosen the steely grip around her ankle. She lashed and kicked out and managed to wrench her leg free from the man's grasp. As soon as she attempted to scuttle away, the man grabbed hold of both her ankles and practically lifted her up, pulling her in towards him.

Clyde clawed at the ground, attempting to slow her captor. Her hands raked troughs in the mud as she was yanked backwards. The force of the pull was jarring, causing her lower back to snap with a new strain of pain, this time one that felt as if her muscles there were being torn apart, the nerves wide open and searing. She twisted about, reaching with one arm down her side, her hand scuttling for the weapon she thought she still had.

She felt a slick tickle of cold metal beneath her fingertips, much to her surprise and relief. The hatchet was still bound there in the makeshift sheath. She supposed the brute that was dragging her had been too distracted to realize she'd still been armed. In any case, there was no time to wonder about the oblivious idiocy of the big man.

All that mattered was that Clyde still had the hatchet.

She used those precious few seconds before she was pulled into the maw of the barn to quickly loosen and then slide the hatchet from its sheath, tucking it beneath her, holding it against her chest. When she had cradled it there, hidden from view, she felt the hands release her legs, letting them drop, striking the dusty threshing floor.

She lay prone on the floor like a ragdoll that had been tossed aside by a petulant child. "Playin' possum," as the locals would call it, she surmised. There was something quaint about its appropriateness, especially in the moment. Clyde stayed still there, face down on the floor, breathing in wafts of dust and taking care not to cough. Her eyes grew itchy with the tickle as she kept the cough down. One slight movement from her, revealing she was alert, and that would be it for her.

She'd done this many times before during her teenaged years up at the Great House, allowing her hours indoors away from the other girls who'd spend the time practicing their shooting, their gunshots loud cracks that tore through the morning, sounding akin to a battlefield. Clyde hadn't liked firearms, even though she, like many of her sisters there, had been a proficient sharpshooter. She preferred the sleek quiet of the blade, and if they could be dipped in any sort of available poison, all the better. She'd taught a few of her sisters a painful, lasting lesson or two during practice sessions in the Silent Room, and they'd not even been aware it had been by her hand. Their hands and faces swelled, their breathing shallow. Only the Quartermaster, who had always prepared the room for them, had the slightest inkling as to the culprit, but even he wasn't entirely certain, for Clyde quickly and deftly fell back among her group, just another stoic face with a doll's prim mouth and blank eyes. They had learned to disappear long before, and by then, Clyde had become a master of invisibility.

Now, that sort of invisibility didn't come easily for her. She liked fashion and high society, beautiful clothing and promenade strolls more than she did vanishing into obscurity. Such foolishness of her contemporaries, who were nothing more than bland wives apt to lose themselves in the dust. She'd chosen the mad gent purposefully, much to the Governess' blatant dismay. The Commodore had enjoyed her dry wit and impeccable manners in her letters, and Clyde had taken note of everything he revealed in his own, from what was said, to the obvious implications, right down to the pauses in his writing that revealed more of his character, and his illness, than any thoughtful rhetoric would provide.

Clyde had brought her poison if she needed it. She had been given careful instructions from the Quartermaster to use it only as a desperate measure, if she was truly alone among the savagery and her life was in mortal peril. Her intent was to tame them though, like the wild beasts they were, and the Governess considered anything remotely deemed as "mortal peril" as a sign of the weak-willed.

That said, whatever the blade, with or without a venom tip, it would work just as well for Clyde. There in that moment in the murderous family's barn, the hatchet and anything else she had available would be perfectly suitable. While the brute was in the midst of his searching, judging by the sounds of his stomping around, rummaging and rustling through whatever it was he was looking for, Clyde waited patiently, listening, her senses alive.

As soon as she gauged the scuffling sounds were far enough away, coming from the darkened depths of the building, Clyde slowly uncoiled, drawing herself up silently from the floor. She turned, her hand with the hatchet unfurling, arm stretching out, her grip tight around the handle.

Her eyes had grown acclimated to the dim light coming from the barn's lone lantern. She wasn't a stranger to the dark. At the Great House, she had trained in darkness for hours until daylight broke. Once, she and her sisters had been taken to the deepest part of the woods at the edge of the estate, all of them blindfolded, and then set loose there, having been told they would need to work together to find their way back. One girl screamed in agony, the Matron who'd escorted them there having cracked the switch against the girl's body. When the Matron snapped at the girl to keep her hands from her face, they realized they would be observed during their test and viciously punished if they attempted to remove their blindfolds.

By the time Clyde and her sisters reached the back gates, worn with exhaustion, mouths parched and stomachs on fire, several of them had been flogged during their grueling journey for daring to reach for their blindfold. Those girls had scars that would never properly heal, and as a result, their suitor selections would be slim. One of them, a girl who would sneak out extra hunks of johnnycake (a preparatory selection purposefully hardened and dry so as to give the experience that special dose of "authenticity" the Governess demanded of Cook), was unable to sit down in her seat at the table for days, her backside in agony. Another lost an eye to a particularly vicious crack to the face, one that rendered the eye seeping with pus and useless. Both girls stayed behind in the employ of the estate, a demotion that rendered them little more than servants in the eyes of the Governess.

Clyde promised herself she would never be weak and lose her way, no matter what happened whether en route to Idlecreek or within the town itself. She considered herself ready for most anything, prepared for the worst.

That aside, she never once thought trouble would find form in her station hosts, whoever they were.

Whatever they were.

Savages.

The brute's colossal frame was a dark, moving mass in front of the giant bale of hay in the corner near the back wall. He was searching for something, oblivious to what was happening behind him.

Clyde slid the hatchet handle in her grip, holding it at the base so that she could correctly pitch it. She stepped back and then swung her arms loosely at her sides, readying herself, keeping herself squarely aligned with the massive man. The timing of it had to be precise, she knew. She kept the handle pointing directly down at her body, wrapping her hand around it, the blade perpendicular to the backside of the brute. Then she brought the hatchet up slowly, her arm straight, elbow flexing just a bit.

At the exact moment she pitched the hatchet forward and released, there was a sharp crack in the air from behind her, and Clyde felt the searing tongue of a whip lash around her neck, yanking her backwards, sending her hurtling, her face going from pale pink to beet purple as she huffed and wheezed, clawing at the leather binding. Whoever had her bound and suffocating had fallen from the weight of pulling her back, and they continued to pull harder, tightening the whip further.

Clyde felt her bladder go, and for all of the pride she'd had to shed herself of during the entirety of the ordeal, for some reason, in that moment, she was utterly mortified.

After all, she was still a lady at heart.

ELEVEN

TO WATCH HER there, writhing on the floor, *süßes Elend*.

Such sweet misery.

The red lady coughs, chokes, the spittle forming strings from her mouth. Her eyes are pushing out from their sockets, puffing there, tearing from the red. She has soiled herself, and the stench of it is foul.

How such a beautiful woman could easily turn into the wretched thing, twisting on the floor like a fish out of water, struggling for air. She is nothing. *Sie ist gemein.*

Für Vati.

Mutti.

Meine schwester.

Mein brudder. He lies there moaning, reaching for his back. I want to go to him, rid him of the pain. The axe she threw cuts his back, and he cannot remove it, but if he does, surely he will bleed to death. I should end his agony, but the red woman must suffer for what she did first.

Meine family. They deserve this all. I wish they could watch her gasping for her life.

Vile woman. *Sie ist nichts.* Boot dirt. Mud. *Scheisse.*

And she has fouled her dress. As if she had known I wanted it so. It makes me hate her more.

Mutti would often tell us, "Hate is a word reserved for the unsaved, the unredeemable, the unwashed, the unholy. We do not use 'hate' unless we mean what we say. And what do we do with the unholy? We end them with pain."

I would say the red woman is deserving of the agony she's enduring, but I want to see her bleed, parts removed, shoved in her mouth, down her gullet. What I wouldn't give to see her swallow herself alive. Have her choke on her own meat and flesh.

A fitting end for *eine Hexe*. A proper death for a witch.

I wonder if she has another dress in her belongings, something unsullied and as beautiful.

A wan face, one with curious eyes and scarred lips, peered over Clyde as she wheezed and clawed at the whip bound around her neck. The girl looked as if she was examining an insect pinned by a housecat underfoot. Using as much strength as she could muster, the scarred girl sharply pulled at the whip, looped it around her wrist, and yanked Clyde in towards her, drawing the woman into a sitting position against her legs. The girl dug a knee in between Clyde's shoulder blades, using the woman's body as leverage to allow her to pull Clyde in tighter, causing the whip to cut into the flesh of her neck.

This would never do. Not at all. Clyde had already begun to loathe herself for becoming so vulnerable over the course of the evening. And there she was, sheer, hot panic overtaking her, on the brink of succumbing to the pitch, her arms and legs going numb and useless, her breaths coming in agonizingly like she was inhaling fire into her lungs. Her mind was growing foggy, and everything around her there in the barn had grown shapeless and soft, the sounds burbling as if coming from underwater.,

She was rapidly losing focus and would have gladly given in to the endless sleep if it weren't for that tiny spark of clarity hovering there, calling out for her to—

Pay.

Close.

Attention.

You are awake, it said, its voice as her own, grounded, assured. *You are awake, and you have options.*

Her eyes flickered open.

The scarred girl was losing strength in her own arms. Clyde could feel the whip sliding, loosening around her neck. She let out a sharp cough and gasped in sweet, cool, damp air, taking whole breaths deeply into her lungs.

The girl screamed out something wordless, formless, a signal of some kind, the sound of it ringing in Clyde's ears.

And that was quite enough for the lady in red.

Clyde pitched her body forward with force, tipping the girl with her and then causing the girl to let go of the whip as she flipped over Clyde and landed on her back with a hard thud on the dusty floor of the barn. The girl mewled at the jarring pain shooting up her back, but Clyde wasn't finished with her. She placed her boot-clad foot down on the girl's shoulder, grinding it hard against the floor as she slowly unwound the whip from around her neck, the burning abrasion there raw and hot.

The girl shrieked and clawed at Clyde's leg, but the lady in red wouldn't relent. She simply didn't have it in her to do so. Normally, she'd have been quite gentle taking care of such a poor creature as the one spitting at her and twisting there beneath her foot. The girl was practically a child, after all, and Clyde's training never prepared her to hurt someone who was an innocent, one who had to submit to a dangerous adult in order to survive. Clyde even identified with that sort of entrapment, truth be told.

This one, however.

This one would have to learn.

And with that, Clyde released her foot from the girl's shoulder, promptly stomping her foot on the girl's chest with enough force to cause an audible cracking of her ribcage. The girl let out a huff of air, her eyes brimming with tears. Clyde then struck the killing blow, a last stomp over the girl's chest, causing the girl's body to curl in on itself, the chest a cavern of an indentation. Blood ran in a dark stream from the girl's open mouth as she went limp.

Clyde barely had time to lift her foot up from the body when the palm of a broad hand, dry and rough with callouses, enveloped her face, smothering her, and a hard, muscular arm wrapped around her middle, pulling her up and off the floor. The hand over her face smothered her, blocking her airways as it cupped and then flattened tightly over her mouth and nose. A combination of the beast's dusty dance, scuffling the floor as he staggered with her, grunting and whuffling, a boorish symphony of noise.

She let go of the hand covering her face, as it was useless for her to attempt to fight it off while she was weakening once more. Instead, she reached behind him at his back, her hand pawing for the prize. He attempted to shake her arm away, his pants of exertion heavy in her ear. His focus on suffocating her was to Clyde's evident advantage, as he couldn't effectively move her arm away. As a result, she was able to clasp her hand around the hatchet handle and wiggle the blade around, causing it to cut deeply as it twisted into his meaty back.

That was plenty enough for the monster to let go of her face with a howl and reach back behind him to rid himself of her grip. With a sharp tug of her fingers with her other hand, the blades in Clyde's brace then sprung to life, and she drove her arm back into his shoulder. The blades worked their magic, slicing the skin, tendons, and muscle there, and Clyde sawed her arm up and down, ripping at his flesh.

Naturally, it worked. Naturally, it had to.

The monster let go of Clyde, shoving her off him and sending her sprawling to the floor. The wind knocked out of her, Clyde could barely draw herself up to her hands and knees, retching and taking in gulps of air as she did. The monster, cradling his wounded arm, sent a sharp kick squarely in her stomach, causing her to topple and curl inward, crying out. The pain of it radiated through her. Served her right, she supposed, an eye for an eye, boot for a boot.

The monster reached behind and clawed for the hatchet still stuck in his back, and then he pulled at the handle, tugging the blade out carefully. Once he managed to pry it out of him, he tossed it to the floor, grimacing, staggering towards the lady in red who was clenching her belly in agony.

Clyde wouldn't give the giant the satisfaction of hovering over her quivering body, relishing her pain as she suffered on the floor. He took a step closer, within inches of her just as Clyde drew up and kicked out both her feet at his shin with such force, the bone seemed to snap inwards, causing him to come crashing down beside her. His howls rang in her ears as she slid herself in his direction, wincing at the pain shooting through her middle. Clyde crawled over the monster's body, roughly pushing his damaged leg down from his grip. She grasped hold of his broken shin and dug her fingertips deep into it and wiggled it sharply. The monster roared, trying to push her off him, but Clyde had such a tight hold on his leg, it would only serve to exacerbate the injury. He pulled at her hair and pushed at her head, swatting at her, his screams echoing throughout the barn, cutting the night.

Clyde wasn't in any sort of shape to keep him writhing, however, so she took it upon herself to pull up from the floor, warily keeping one eye on the man who was drawing himself up to a sitting position, half-cradling his injured leg, half-pushing back at the floor, working to get himself standing.

The monster was in no shape though, not to move without stumbling, and just as he had wobbled his way up to his feet, there was a whoosh of air, and he was back down again.

The hatchet blade split the top of his skull. The force of the blow Clyde inflicted used her last ounce of strength. Both she and the monster collapsed, she, breathing sharply.

He, finally still.

TWELVE

THE SKY HAD shed itself of its tears. Stars dotted the wide expanse of it, some of them having just awoken, others winking back at the horizon, welcoming the coming dawn. Their wakefulness would be short-lived, but in the time they had left before morning, they could, at least, enjoy themselves for the time being.

And the land had been satiated, having eaten its fill.

The lady in red staggered across the little stretch of land between the barn and stables where the stage horses had been kept during the night. She hoped they'd survived as well, but she didn't know the extent of the family's intent. They'd not been common thieves. The lot of them had taken *pleasure* in what they'd inflicted.

Exactly how many stage passengers had they—

Never mind, Clyde thought. *It didn't matter anyway.*

They were no longer a problem, no longer *her* problem.

She took one look at what was left in the stables— the pulp of Leartus' face, his prone body, the slaughtered horses—and immediately turned back around and headed outside. This time, however, Clyde wandered the wet stretch of pasture aimlessly, her thoughts akimbo as she had no idea what she could possibly do without viable transport. The air felt good against her skin, cool and damp, relaxing her tired muscles and soothing her wounds. If anything, it would clear her mind and get her to focus while she was out in the open, breathing in the aroma of the wet earth.

"Miss Northway, I swear on my mama, you're a plumb sight if ever I seen," said a familiar voice from behind Clyde. A voice that was strangely comforting, yet startling all at once.

She turned to face Moody, who looked as if he'd also been through a hell of a night, and she staggered backwards, stumbling in the muddy earth. Where on earth had he been during her ordeal, she wondered. His right eye was swollen shut, purpling and puffy with blood. His hair was sticking out in tufts. He'd been bludgeoned with something, Clyde surmised from the blood congealing on top of his head. Not hard enough to do much damage though.

Clyde gently touched the wound on his head, causing him to flinch away from her fingers. "You look as if you'd challenged the wrong brute at the right time," she said with an idle chuckle.

Moody returned the grin and winced, regretting it instantly. Clyde saw the dark red gaps in his lower gumline and nodded in sympathy.

"Might I say, you look like you found yourself in the same scenario," he said, motioning a hand in her direction.

"We're a sight, aren't we?"

"We live an' learn, ma'am. We live an' learn."

Clyde stared hard at him for a long moment before she said, "Where on earth did they keep you? Where *were* you, boy?"

"Oh, hell, they had me all hogtied up in one of them bedrooms, plannin' to keep me for one of the girls there. 'Bout beat me senseless when I told 'em I weren't gonna be no stallion for them fuckers." Moody went pink all over as soon as the word came out and looked down at the earth, shaking his head at his own coarseness. "Sorry, Miss Northway. I tend t'get ever firey passionate when I'm out of my mind with heat n' hate."

Clyde simply stood there, still studying him carefully as if she was contemplating what to do with him.

Moody cleared his throat loudly and pointed back towards the other end of the estate. "I got me one of their wagons out front there. They got cattle in the pasture over in that direction. I guess they'd been payin' too much attention to all of us, they done forgot to take them in before it rained. I mean, I'm just presumin' is all. If you wake ol' Leartus up in the barn an' tell him what's been happenin', he can—"

"Mr. Shurchell is as dead as the rest, Mr. Evers, and I don't think either of us has the ability to perform necromancy to wake him. Not that he would be in any condition to perform his role as shotgun. His eyes are useless. There's not much of his face left."

Moody gave her a partial grimace, and it was horrifying to see his own damaged face attempt it. His skin stretched, his abrasions spread, and his wounded eye wept. Clyde put a hand on his shoulder, gave it a gentle squeeze. "We'll be fine, Mr. Evers. It'll just be the two of us this time, I'm afraid."

"Not nobody left then?" he whispered.

"Not a one."

"Not even Mrs. Wilkson? She were pregnant with child."

"I'm sorry."

"Them fuckers."

"Them fuckers indeed, Mr. Evers."

The last of the supplies, what had been stocked in the stables and pantry, along with their belongings, were loaded into the tattered Prairie Schooner, and with quite a degree of difficulty, they managed to yoke and hitch a couple of the sturdier oxen that had suffered through the rainy night in the pasture. The little transport had seen some action over the years as well, apparently, as it seemed to have endured some sort of damage in the midst of what might have been a gunfight as there were telltale bullet holes in its sideboards. Clyde didn't have it in her to be concerned over the mystery of the wagon and its previous riders. All she was concerned with was getting to her destination as safely as she could. It would take a long day's journey to get to Idlecreek, and that was all she needed.

It would have to be a day free of any encounters on the journey, however. They took two shotguns, Mrs. Adlers' derringer, Leartus' prized Smith and Wesson Model 3, and all of the ammunition they could find, which wasn't much, but Clyde presumed it would be perfectly suitable for a day's worth of travel.

The two of them settled in the driver's seat, side by side, Clyde as passenger, with the derringer set in her lap and Moody as the driver. Reins in hand, Moody paused for a moment, reflecting upon something, his gaze focused on the distant landscape.

Clyde's heart rate had begun to escalate in its temperament. She sat there, perfectly still and collected though, waiting patiently for Moody to say whatever it was he needed to say.

"Ask you somethin', Miss Northway?"

She cleared her throat, closed her eyes for a second, then opened them. Breathed. "Certainly," she said, her voice steady, belying her racing heart.

"It's a mite embarrassin'."

"We've no time for idle chat, you know."

"Oh, forgive me, ma'am, but this . . . it's kinda important to me s'all, an' I wouldn't trouble you none if I didn't have to . . . but I do."

Clyde's fingers curled in her lap. Her breath went still.

Moody slowly turned to look directly at her. "I really and truly do, you understand. You *must* understand. You bein' a lady n'all. An' you an' me. We now got us somethin' in common, somethin' we now share. We don't got family no more, do we? But at least . . . at *least* you're gettin' ready for a new life . . . with a new husband. An' that man's gonna take good care of you."

Her body went stiff all over.

"So you don't have need for nothin' fancy now, do you? You're gonna have all the dresses sent from all over, ain't you? *Vati* would've wanted me to have a dress. I figured it's only fair, it's only right, *Fraulein* Northway. All my life . . . All I wanted was to please my father, but we needed another boy. *They* needed another boy. I been a boy ever since, doin' my duty, bringing them travelers with their money *und ihre Kleider und Juwelen*. Bringing them fancies. And every day, every single day, *mein Vati* promised me I could be as beautiful as I was meant to be. I'd be—"

But Moody Evers, or whatever his or her actual name had been at some point in his miserable life, had his words cut short when he suddenly found himself with a mouthful of blades ripping the inside of his maw, sawing his lips, his gums, the skin around his mouth, shredding it all to stringy, red, viscous ribbons. His eyes went round and teary in shock, his nostrils twitching.

Before he could make a sound, Clyde ripped the bladed brace from his mouth and then drove it back into his face, impaling it with the blades. She wrenched the brace out again, the blades taking slices of skin, meat, and the jelly of a lone eyeball with it. His face now a shredded mess of gore and gristle, Moody could only manage a gurgling sound.

Clyde put Moody to rest by promptly picking up the derringer and firing it into the side of his skull.

The oxen rumbled, their snorts relaying their unease.

And with that, Clyde shushed the beasts, soothing them as she calmly set the derringer beside her. She waited a good minute before shoving Moody's body off the seat and onto the ground. She slid over in the seat, took the reins in hand, and drove off.

The sun coming up over the horizon painted the world with such clarity.

It was such a pity Clyde Northway couldn't find it in her to enjoy much of anything, not even a beautiful sunrise. After all, she was coming into town to meet her new husband, the Commodore, looking, quite frankly, like the devil in what was once a really lovely red dress.

ACKNOWLEDGEMENTS

Special thanks to . . .

. . . Kevin Wallace, Rebecka Ramos, Mike Ennenbach, and Lucy Spencer for bravely offering to lend an eye.

. . . Patrick C. Harrison III and Jarod Barbee for crafting a fantastic concept, for bringing an amazing group of authors together, and for their absolute patience with me.

. . . Justin T. Coons for the fantastic cover design.

. . . Jeff Strand for his unwavering mentorship and friendship.

. . . and the horror community for their kindness in welcoming the likes of me into the fold.

ABOUT THE AUTHOR

Kenzie Jennings is an English professor living in the sweltering tourist hub of central Florida. She is the author of the Splatterpunk nominated cannibal wedding novel *Reception* (Death's Head Press). Her short horror fiction has appeared in *Worst Laid Plans: An Anthology of Vacation Horror, Dig Two Graves, Vol. 1* and *Deep Fried Horror: Mother's Day Edition.*